Annie Macdonell

Thomas Hardy

Annie Macdonell

Thomas Hardy

ISBN/EAN: 9783337395766

Printed in Europe, USA, Canada, Australia, Japan

Cover: Foto ©Raphael Reischuk / pixelio.de

More available books at **www.hansebooks.com**

BY

ANNIE MACD

LONDON

DDER & STOUGH

27 PATERNOSTER ROW

1894

CONTENTS

CONTENTS

CHAPTER VII

CHAPTER VIII

CHAPTER IX

CHAPTER X

Contemporary Writers

Edited by W. ROBERTSON NICOLL, LL.D.

THOMAS HARDY

INTRODUCTORY

INTRODUCTORY

E can be no attempt at finality in
icism of Mr. Hardy: he is now in
ull vigour of his genius, and he has
prepared us for surprises. But the
e of his work is already large; and
is a natural delight in counting and
a heap of treasure, even though the
being added to while our hands are in
d its net value being possibly altered.
if this—be it personal gratification, or
homage to the source of the treasure—
reason enough for one more attempt
praise it, I have no other. Mr. Hardy
id: he needs no explanation; no
y: his work can defend itseif; and

he has probably all the popularity he desires. But he presents abundance of points for study, and though his unexpected developments have been many, and his caprices not a few, some distinctive features are clearly enough traceable from his earliest to his most recent page to prevent a criticism of his work being a thing of shreds and patches.

Touching and influencing the main streams of art and thought to-day at certain points, at others standing far apart from them, Mr. Hardy holds just now a position of special interest ; and in the long line of English novelists his is a noticeable figure. He has made really new departures which are no mere accidents of the day he has lived in ; he has resisted some impulses of his time as sturdily as in other directions he has been a revolutionary. You may quote him as an example of the observance, and as a warning against the breach, of the same canons of criticism if you happen to hold with any. He is that interesting subject, a writer that cannot be labelled. Ready-made theories about realism, naturalism, and romanticism, are misfits as applied to him : his methods are as wayward as the loves of his heroines.

In spite of the modern habit of diligently searching for a writer's literary parentage, a criticism of Mr. Hardy may start from himself. The sun and wind of other minds shone and blew on him, of course, and fed his growth, and there are marks for all who read closely that certain men and books have left on him strong imprints. But he has been nobody's docile pupil. He has disciplined himself well in thinking and observing, and his eye and ear are naturally quick and true. But for style and form, pattern and tone, he has gone to school just when and where he liked. The worse for the smoothness of the web, and its value among dealers who judge by rule of thumb. But there are other tests.

Among the many blunders that line the path of the random art of literary criticism, perhaps none has been more unintelligent than that which attributed Mr. Hardy's first widely-known story to George Eliot. The guess seems wild now, but the notion still remains that her influence was great in the shaping of his literary methods. So it may have been : it is a point better settled by information than by internal evidence, which is far from distinct. In a few instances his humour looks as if it had meant to be after a George Eliot pattern, but had turned out something entirely different. The best novels of both have rustic backgrounds ; both have made prominent the speech and humours of English peasants ; both are marked by a strong intellectual fibre. But in aim, style, and temperament, it would be difficult to name two writers of fiction more dissimilar. And of no other novelist does he call up a clear remembrance : certainly no very pro-fitable comparison can be made between him and his contemporaries. In one point, in his representation of the ceaseless warring of human nature with itself and fatal circumstance, his final aim, he puts us in mind of Balzac, and as soon as the likeness is named the great differences in their methods rise up to obscure it.

Kinship he has with other writers, but they are not writers of fiction, and they are of another time than ours. He has borrowed; but his borrowings have been open and audacious. Where he is not looking with his own peculiarly independent gaze at the world, it is nobody less than Shakespeare that has lent him eyesight. This, of course, does not affect Mr. Hardy's rank in literature: whatever it may be he has earned it by other qualities than skill in adaptation. Nor has it reference to the fact that the novelist at his supremest moments is a tragedian. It is Shakespeare's lighter vein, as 'fancy's child,' that the skill of the storyteller has adapted to the interpretation of an

England two and a half centuries older.
Some of Mr. Hardy's much loved and exas-
perating heroines are Shakespearian. His
rustics are of his own Wessex soil, but perhaps Shakespeare gave him the courage and
example to extract and distil their wit in defiance of what stands for probability in minds
of conventional experience. Fancy, a rare
quality, plays out and in persistently amid
the gloomiest scenes of the Wessex stories ;
for the novelist of to-day whose final aim
points most clearly to the tragedy of life, is
yet the one of all others who best recalls that
the careless airy brightness of an earlier world
is unexhausted yet—a brightness, by the by,
having nothing to do with happiness, being
rather a gleam of outside sunshine, elfish and
irresponsible, taking little account of the
reason for living or of its futility, but very
nearly concerned with its possibility.

Mr. Hardy began his literary career with
a stock of thoughts and a view of life considerably in advance of, or different from, those

of the majority of his contemporaries. The
distinctly intellectual quality of his genius
has hardly been adequately recognised, and
indeed this feature is apt to be ignored in a
novelist, save where it is out of proportion
to the imaginative powers, as in the case of
George Eliot. Fearless thinking and a sense
of humour having been his from the first, he
has rarely been taken unawares and captured
by the fashions and crazes among his fellow-
craftsmen at any moment. In his time we
have had the psychological, the historico-
romantic, the neurotic, the erotic, the photo-
graphic, and many another school, and each
has looked on itself as the advance guard.
Mr. Hardy has contributed to more than
one, and joined none. Yet he is still,
admittedly, in England, the leader into freer
paths. Peculiarly unprofessional in tone, he
never echoes the literary club, coterie, or
review, and in a generation fussily proud of
all its little efforts at thinking, which makes
continual discovery of problems, and many

solemn statements of them, he has not very often worn his serious purposes on his sleeve. But you will find good thought and earnestness wrought closely into the fibre of his work—enough of these to bar his way to any very wide popularity—and he has impressively dramatised a problem or two, neither particularly new nor old, but of a kind to be met with so long as our present civilisation lasts. Now standing aloof from the time, and again its ally, but never enrolled in the regular army, he has been a valiant freelance.

PROGRESS OF A NOVELIST

I

II

THE PROGRESS OF A
NOVELIST

I

THOMAS HARDY was born near Dorchester, June 2, 1840, and he lives in Dorchester now. That only a little portion of his life has been spent away from that neighbourhood is the most significant fact of his biography. Wessex, with its natural beauty, its remoteness, its lingering old world customs, has been not merely a picturesque background to his tales. They have grown in Wessex air, and he has dug them out of Wessex soil. In most other novels the scenery could be altered with little effect on the action or the characters. In Mr. Hardy's it is always inevitable and organic. There has been in recent years a strong revival of local sentiment, and folk-lore, fiction, and pictorial art have reflected it. The very restlessness of modern life has nourished a love for some abiding-place, where the heart and the imagination can turn to for a home and for repose; and regret for the old world so quickly passing away has inspired many picturesque chroniclers. The spirit of nationalism, one of the strongest motive-powers of the century, has had this as its local counterpart. But Mr. Hardy's attachment, and his choice of habitation for the creatures of his imagination, are almost too personal to be set down to the contagion of a movement. White has not Selborne more precisely in his eye; Wordsworth has not with greater love interpreted the soul of the hills and lakes he was born amongst; Burns and Ayrshire have not a closer association. And no other

writer of fiction has been at once so truthful and so poetic a historian of his county.
You will more easily find a parallel among
painters than among men of letters.

It was perhaps fortunate that Mr. Hardy's
education enabled him to be early obedient
to his own instincts. He could never have
been one of the 'hall-marked young men,'
lightly satirised by himself, one of 'the un-
impeachable models turned out yearly by
the lathe of a systematic tuition': his humanity and originality would always have
been stronger than his education. With a
strictly conventional training he might have
been more of the man of letters; he might
have been considerably less of the dramatist
of life. In his seventeenth year he was
articled to an ecclesiastical architect in
Dorchester, and the traces of this apprentice-
ship, and of his studies for his profession,
are plainly evident in his writing, in the
precision with which he describes a building
or a neighbourhood, and notes position,

distance, and proportion. Very probably it
strengthened his love of pictorial art, and in-
directly had not a little to do with the fact
that he comes nearer to having the vision
and using the methods of a painter than
any other novelist one could name. His
work, too, gave him roving errands about
the county—when he stored another kind
of capital than professional skill—for to his
master had been entrusted the restoration
of many of the old South Dorsetshire
churches.

But architecture did not, even in those
early days, absorb all his thoughts and
energies, and for the next four years he was
a diligent student of literature, more especially of classics and theology. At the age
of twenty Mr. Hardy came to London, to
pursue his profession, and there attached
himself to the modern Gothic school, working under the distinguished architect Sir
Arthur Blomfield, and helping him in the
restoration of several churches in the neigh-

bourhood of London. Sir Arthur Blomfield is painter as well as architect, and probably his influence over his pupil was still more in the direction of fostering his love of art than of training him in design. In 1863, the prize and medal of the Institute of British Architects was awarded to the competitor who wrote, under the motto, ' Tentavi quid ' in congenere possem,' an essay on ' Col- ' oured Brick and Terra Cotta Architecture.' This was Mr. Hardy's first public success, and in the same year he received Sir W. Tite's prize for architectural design. These are all his recorded separate efforts in his early profession, though he continued to pursue it seriously for some years, and the final choice between architecture and litera- ture was probably not made till 1874.

On his arrival in London he had entered as a student of modern languages at King's College, and side by side with his profession literature was asserting claims on his time and interest. A little paper, ' How I built

myself a House,' which appeared in
Chambers' Journal, in 1865, is probably his
first published work.   It is not technical,
as might be supposed from its title, but a
slight and humorous sketch of the experience of two enthusiastic young house-
keepers, with awful warnings as to ex-
penses and unexpected happenings in the
dangerous amusement of house-building.
But the leisure of the years that elapsed
between his coming to London and the
publication of his first novel was devoted
to poetry, not to fiction.   There is probably more in this than the mere conventional beginning of almost every literary
career.   Mr. Hardy is first of all a poet, if
his other gifts and ambitions sometimes
tend to obscure the fact, and though the
world has not had much chance of gauging
his skill in metrical form.   Publishers
behaved just as usual, and made no eager
move to welcome another young man's
verses.   The album verse in ' Desperate

Remedies ' is not his only metrical com-
position in print, but the magazines were not
very hospitable to what consumed the best
ardour of Mr. Hardy's mind for several
years; and the book of poems that has
been so frequently the future prose writer's
introduction to the world, in his case mostly
remained in manuscript.

At last he took to novel-writing, and
' Desperate Remedies ' was published anonymously, by Messrs. Tinsley, in 1871.
Though it had its share of abuse, its reception was such as to place him within the
first outposts of success. But his years of
patient training, and his observant youth in
Wessex, had soon a finer result. By one of
the unaccountable leaps, some backward,
some forward, which have marked Mr.
Hardy's progress, this vigorous but somewhat awkward story was followed, a year
after, by another, which for beauty of workmanship and charm he has never surpassed,
' Under the Greenwood Tree.' ' A Pair of

Blue Eyes' appeared in 1873. It was not, however, till the practically unqualified success in 1874 of 'Far from the Madding Crowd,' which appeared in *Cornhill* in that year, that Mr. Hardy's career seemed to be finally settled. Five years later this novel, perhaps, not even excepting 'Tess,' the most popular of his works, was dramatised by himself. A version of it, written in collaboration with Mr. Comyns Carr, in which occur some modifications of the plot, was performed, in February 1882, at the Prince of Wales's Theatre, Liverpool, Miss Marion Terry playing Bathsheba, that part being taken by Mrs. Bernard Beere when it appeared on the London stage, at the Globe, in May of the same year. His only other dramatised work is 'The Three Wayfarers,' based on 'The Three Strangers,' one of the 'Wessex Tales,' performed, with four other one act plays, at Terry's Theatre in June 1893.

Since his renunciation of architecture his

literary life has not been spent in London. Returning to Wessex he finally settled at Dorchester, where he now lives. Mr. Hardy's developments may yet be many, and only one thing can be foreseen with any degree of certainty, that Wessex will still be the stage where his dramas will play. Not only has he old memories to fall back on and suggest his scenes and stories: by choice, all his present working days are spent where Wessex cannot be out of sight or mind. Just below him, on the north, lies the Frome Valley, with glimpses of the wild heath country beyond; towards the sea, Blackdown with his namesake's monument stands conspicuous to the right; nearer on the same side are the great ramparts of Mai-Dun, and in front the rolling downs of 'The Trumpet Major.'

There he has written with regularity, but not too prolifically, the order of his works, after those already named, being, 'The Hand of Ethelberta,' 1876; 'The Return of the

Native,' 1878 ; 'The Trumpet Major,' 1880 ;
'A Laodicean,' 1881 ; 'Two on a Tower,'
1882 ; 'The Mayor of Casterbridge,' 1886 ;
'The Woodlanders,' 1886-7 ; 'Wessex
Tales,' 1888 ; 'A Group of Noble Dames,'
1891 ; 'Tess of the D'Urbervilles,' 1892 ;
'The Pursuit of the Well-Beloved,' 1892 :
'Life's Little Ironies,' 1894. Mr. Hardy
has been also an infrequent contributor
to periodical literature in other directions
than fiction. Among his more notable
articles are, one on 'The Dorset Labourer '
in *Longman's Magazine* of July 1893—an
interesting commentary on the material
for the Wessex novels, and an obituary
notice of the Rev. William Barnes,
the Dorset poet, which appeared in the
Athenæum of October 16, 1886. Barnes
was his near neighbour—two fields only
divide his house from the rectory of Winterborne Came—and the difference in age,
temperament, and point of view, did nothing
to prevent a warm friendship between the

two men who, each in his own way, have finely interpreted the life and character of the county they have both loved so well. Dorset has been singularly fortunate in the loyalty as in the gifts of two such sons.

THE PROGRESS OF A
NOVELIST

II

III

THE PROGRESS OF A
NOVELIST

II

THE republication of 'Desperate Remedies'
in 1892 gave a new and wider circulation
to Mr. Hardy's earliest work of fiction.
Markedly unlike most of the later books
in its surface tones, the difference is yet
mainly one of season rather than of climate;
and as the story contains the germs of almost every idea, talent, and tendency to be
found in his work since its appearance, it
is as worthy of close attention as some of
the better books.

'Desperate Remedies' was published

anonymously in 1871. On its title-page it bore a quotation from Scott, a manifesto in defence of its construction rather than a motto,—'Though an unconnected course of adventures is what most frequently occurs in nature, yet the province of the romance-writer being artificial, there is more required from him than a mere compliance with the simplicity of reality.' And indeed he has selected, arranged, and adapted the events with much thoroughness. It is a story of plot and sensation, the incidents precisely adjusted to a complicated plan, workman-like rather than attractive, the novel of one who, making up his mind to construct an elaborate plot, straightway did it without bungling or breakdown, but not with the convincing success of an equally complicated story of sensation, say, by Wilkie Collins. A feature, or perhaps, a freak of the book, its divisions into sections headed, 'The Events of Thirty Years,' 'The Events of a Fortnight,' 'The Events of a Day and a

Night,' and so on, has a look of being part of the painstaking plan. Whatever its intention, it serves but a slight purpose, though it marks a precision which Mr. Hardy afterwards transferred, and with greater effect, from time to place. It is also a novel of character; there are no puppets, though some of the more important personages are a little rigid in their movements. A Wessex story, the rustic humours and humourists, to many readers the most prominent feature of Mr. Hardy's tales, are here already, and Clerk Crickett, the 'kind of Bowdlerised rake,' is surpassed by few of the later wits.

The frankness of conception and of language, more or less a determined purpose all along, begàn in this earliest novel. The story turns largely on the secret breach of the social code of morality by a young and inexperienced woman, who afterwards came to such a position as made the discovery of her secret dangerous; on her contrivance to introduce her unrecognising son into her employment; and her resolve to effect a marriage between him and the daughter of a later, honourable, and disappointed lover. The design, joined in by Manston, the son, who has already a wife, leads to deep plotting and eventually to murder. Such a story can hardly be called agreeable, but the insistence is on the dramatic action rather than on the sordid detail of the tragedy. In the recent edition there has been considerable verbal revision, for the most part unimportant, the Bowdlerisation of a word or two not being of a character to give any particular interest to the earlier version. The complacency with life and the tragic despair of it that mark most young men's novels are both absent, an austere facing of its ills taking their place. In the melodramatic parts even, a firm intellectual grip of life is felt, and the philosophy not dramatised into situations or characters, if a trifle wordily expressed, is firsthand and never flimsy. A Nature painter of the rarest kind he proved himself from the beginning, and the love of picturesque circumstance which has inspired some of his greatest moments, as it has also allied itself on less fortunate occasions to melodrama, is already a feature. In a story where sorrow and evil assert themselves in their full power, and with a forbidding aspect, the little scene is gratefully remembered where, on Cytherea's wedding-day with Manston, she and Spring-rove touch hands and bid farewell with the flowing stream between them. The style is vigorous and ambitious, but it is also that of a bookish man whose pen has not gained agility. It is a style that Mr. Hardy re-adopts from time to time, suggesting con-scientious drill more than spontaneous exer-cise; it is the language of dissertation and exposition rather than of art.

Such is the novel Mr. Hardy first sent out to the world, for the material in it, for its throughness and grip, remarkable in itself, but specially interesting read in the light

of the later work. For a first book by an
anonymous writer, it was not received
badly. Indeed the *Saturday* welcomed it
with enthusiasm. It was dubbed 'unplea-
sant' but 'powerful' by another leading
organ of literary opinion, the reviewer being
a little puzzled as to the sex of the writer,
though he hoped it was not by 'an English
lady.' For a certain outspokenness of language it was duly reproved.

'Under the Greenwood Tree' is called on
its title-page, 'A Rural Picture of the Dutch
School,' and there is in it a good deal of the
vigorous trust in homely detail that reminds
one of Jan Steen and Van Ostade. But the
transcript has been made by a poet's hand.
To not a few the book appears as Mr.
Hardy's surest claim to recognition in another age, inasmuch as it is least coloured
by the dusty complexion of ours. All but
flawless in workmanship, its tone and humour are of the kindliest. Nature and human
nature, in sleepy woodland hamlets, are

seen, not with the vagueness of a roving
lover of the picturesque, but with an eye
that has noted how the light falls upon the
leaves at all the hours and all the seasons,
and read the minutest meaning of the smiles
that play round rustic lips. You may put it
on the shelf with the 'Vicar of Wakefield'
and Walton and 'As You Like It,' but its
piquancy will make it best neighbour to the
last. It is an untraditional idyll: Arcadia
with a savour.

For all the intimacy with rural habit and
character it reveals, Mr. Hardy is not
amongst the literalists. 'Under the Greenwood Tree' is the picture of a mood, of the
conscious glee and the unconscious humour
of country life, a mood of which the sum is
large enough, counted by the broken experiences of it in every country heart, but which
needs, as well as a light hand to paint it, an
eye that can divert itself for a time from yesterday's pain and the view of to-morrow's drud-
gery, and see it as it exists to each, at happy

C

times, the sole mood of all the world. The
story bubbles over with pure fun; its romance
is as fresh and gentle as a spring morning.
It is the comedy of country life meeting its
lighter poetry. The shadows lying outside
the sunny spot never obtrude. You can't
make a tragedy out of Fancy's 'I like Dick,
' and I love him; but how poor and mean a
' man looks in the rain, with no umbrella,
' and wet through!' and you needn't out
of 'those beautiful eyes of hers—too refined
' and beautiful for a tranter's wife; but,
' perhaps, not too good.' And the shadow
creeps no nearer among the leaves and
scents of Yalbury wood and the sunshine
of simple hearts, amid the buzz of cottage
mirth and the twang of fiddles at Christmas
merry-makings.

'A Pair of Blue Eyes' is not a Wessex
novel, the scene lying in a remote Cornish
parish and in London. Sophisticated folks
play parts in it, and play them indifferently.
It holds its place in readers' affections by its

strange love story, by the vagaries of the heroine, and the genuine unaccented pathos of the end. Elfride is one of Mr. Hardy's special maidens. Whatever her deservings, she is remembered by readers as she is treated by her creator, with the tenderness called out by beautiful things that die young. A charming child, who 'says things worthy ' of a French epigrammatist, and acts like a ' robin in a greenhouse,' she has the variableness of a subtle nature and the promise of a woman of passion; she fibs, makes terrible mistakes, and yet deserves somehow by her nature, if not by her acts, the love of the three men who mourned over her in the Luxellian family vault. It is a story of memorable scenes, and with much beauty in the circumstances and the setting. The tragic note of the battle with the inevitable in nature is first struck here with a deep sound. Technically less elaborate, it is still, from a craftsman's point of view, a great advance on 'Desperate Remedies,' to which it seems naturally the successor, and it stirs one's sympathies much more readily and lastingly.

Turning back now to 'A Pair of Blue Eyes,' its most interesting feature is seen to be the foreshadowing in it of Angel Clare's part in Tess's tragedy. Knight, though a priggish London reviewer, is a robuster, if less picturesque figure than Angel: but their point of view is the same. Personally Knight had a better case for himself, but according to social conventions, in spite of Elfride's fibs, he had less cause for his prudish cruelty. The situation wants the tragic circumstances that occur in 'Tess'; otherwise it is the same: the casting off of the warmest love by a man who finds that an earlier story, into which he did not enter, contains what does not fit in with his conventional code for the ideal of womankind.

Perhaps 'Far from the Madding Crowd' is still, as it was for long, the most popular of Mr. Hardy's stories, in spite of the fact that it exemplifies all the qualities, though

not all of them at their strongest, by which
he has given offence. When it appeared in
book form, his name for the first time on a
title-page, his recognition as a writer of un-
usual vigour was immediate ; it was a recognition, nevertheless, modified by so much
criticism, that the succeeding books had still
to fight their way. It presents a greater
variety of moods than any of the others. The
range and room of English country life for
purposes of fiction he first proved in this
story, which is at once comedy, tragedy,
idyll, rustic chronicle, and shepherd's calendar. Into no other book has he put such
close and lavish work ; none is more viva
cious, more characteristic ; it contains the
essence of his genius. In reading it first of
all—and it has introduced Mr. Hardy to
many—you have the feeling of crossing or
climbing something before reaching the level
of full appreciation, a sensation to some extent, of course, marking every first acquaintance with a writer of originality. The feeling

is not experienced in the same degree in any of the other novels. His individuality lies in his 'humour,' to use the word in its older sense, in his love for the unexpected, the impulsive, the vivid, in human nature and incident, in his delight in upsetting the minor proprieties, and making mock of the solemnity of petty conventions. Bathsheba's prank of sending the valentine to Boldwood is typical of this somewhat impish temper. His 'humour' is what those critics have in mind who accuse him of a want of taste. There is something bristling in Mr. Hardy; there is little or no placidity; and not only in his defiant temper do you feel this. His very virtues add to the effect, the vividness of his pictures, the complex interest of his characters, the heat of the emotions he expresses. He is always awake and strenuous; there is hardly a comfortable sleepy corner in one of his stories. Perhaps that is why he jars on some nerves, though his holding the conventions as mostly of little account has been his chief cause of offence. In his novels the middle classes have their due share of representation, and I do not call to mind any passage in which he has gibed at them, or treated them otherwise than honourably. But he is not their novelist. The calm orderliness, the prudence, the respectability—the conditions by which they keep their comfortable position—are not the qualities he finds most interesting. Bathsheba so typifies his unconventionality in minor matters that 'Far from the Madding Crowd' is an excellent starting-point for making his nearer acquaintance, apart from the fact that it represents his powers at their full compass, though not at their mellowest.

In 'The Hand of Ethelberta,' a London and a Wessex story, light satire is the prevailing note. If the Society scenes are not admirable, they, at least, provide the contrast that makes the piquant comedy in the history of the heroine. Ethelberta is the daughter of a highly respectable family

butler, shoved up into an equality with the
great folks whom her father waits on, by her
graces and talents more even than by her
marriage with an aristocratic minor who died
in their honeymoon. For the sake of a
numerous band of lowly brothers and sisters
she fights for position, and lives in a perpetual conspiracy to hide or disguise their
existence and the other *postscenia vitae* for
the sake of that same position. The much
sought lady of many suitors, her difficulties
never give her heart a chance, and she ends
as the wife of an old noble rake. The
bitterness of the facts is hardly expressed in
the tone, and the underside of the beautiful
and vivacious Ethelberta, a dogged family
faithfulness, keeps her history wholesome.
A very lively story is made out of the shifts
of the household which she rules as mistress,
and where brother Joey is page-boy, and sisters Gwendoline and Cornelia are cook and
housemaid, and out of the contrasts of her
two lives, one spent in regulating the minutest

details of the life of her humble family, the other in charming London drawing-rooms by her poems and wit. The Anglebury rustics, as well as the Chickerel family, supply humorous by-play, and the London scenes some smart gibes at fashionable frigidities. Here, as in 'A Pair of Blue Eyes,' the weary strife against the senseless class feeling in English society is dramatised, but true to the note struck in the sub-title, 'A Comedy in Chapters,' and to the essentially practical nature of the heroine, neither this struggle nor the worldly marriage that ends it is presented in a tragic light. On the whole it is an amusing story, rising occasionally to brilliancy. Wherever the scenes are not merely conventional they are full of vigour: the journey of the Honourable Edgar and Sol Chickerel, builder, together into Wessex, each determined to prevent a *mésalliance*, the one of a noble brother to a beautiful low-born adventuress, the other of a beloved, if remotely understood, sister, to an old rakish

aristocrat, candidly uncivil fellow-travellers,
compelled by desperate necessity to act together even to the joint frying of bacon in
their forced stopping-place, is one of the
finest bits of narrative in all the stories.

Then came a book which gathered up the
undertones of much of Mr. Hardy's previous
work. But in 'The Return of the Native'
they are no longer undertones, but swelled,
concentred, and urged into burning, tense,
and reverberating expression.   They are
never long absent from the later work, but
their fullest articulation is in this book that
misses just criticism and nice valuation by its
tremendous appeal to sympathies which are
either knit in with the very fibres of life, or
remote, or non-existent.   It is a tragedy of
temperaments ; it is likewise one in which
Nature and man have that rare but always
fateful meeting where they wholly blend or
endlessly struggle.   Sea and moorland are
the everlasting plains where such meetings
take place, where Nature aggressively pits

herself against man, or receives his fullest
allegiance; and never have the battle and
the blending been more hauntingly pictured
than in this story of Egdon Heath. The
great struggle of Lear on the same wild land
is more of an incident in another kind of
tragedy. Here the heath has a personality,
a temperament, far more forcible than any
of its dwellers; it is a brooding, pervasive
presence acting on them always, stinging
them to revolt, encircling and hushing them.
One forgets willingly enough the incidents
of the story, to remember it only as the expression of the dark, resisting, untameable
mood of nature, set to a human tune.

Society has been left far behind, which
never means with Mr. Hardy—or any one
else not tainted with literary west-end pro-
vincialism—the absence in the characters of
complex human motives. Outer and inner
experiences are by no means always coex-
tensive. One of the principal actors is a son
of the soil, who has left Paris and worldly

success to find something better to do than selling trinkets in a suffering world, and who comes back to the heath to find his work, which he does, first in furze-cutting, and eventually in preaching. The other is an exotic, perfervid woman, craving the light and glitter of the outer world, with an original brain and a mean soul, made tragic by her terribly alien circumstances. They are not ordinary characters, but they are as likely to be found on a heath as elsewhere, and when they are, a tragedy is in the making. 'The Return of the Native' is the old tale of the new, the slight, the vulgar, struggling against the old, the strong, the real; of passion warring, now against passion and now against thought; of ambition and idealism in their ever futile striving. Round about like wild-flowers growing in blithe confidence on the edge of a roaring torrent, are the quaint humours, the unthinking repose, of Grandfer Cantle, of Christian, and the mummers. It is a book of striking incidents and

powerful dramatic situations, but it is easy
to find blemishes and incongruities in it.
'Wuthering Heights,' though it outrages human probabilities far more in its characters,
has, in the simplicity and boldness of its construction, a great advantage over this kindred
book. Both are poems rather than novels ;
but 'The Return of the Native' has the
ambition to be completely a novel, too, and
the narrative is not always on a level with the
spirit enwrapping it—a spirit that were more
fittingly set to a wild metre and music. The
youthful mood of the world was reflected
in 'Under the Greenwood Tree'; 'The
Return of the Native' reflects, not the aged,
perhaps, which may be less sensitive and
gentler, but rather maturity, with its emotions
at their strongest, and its eyes at their
full courage, looking unshrinkingly on the
struggle at its darkest and bitterest. Mr.
Hardy has written cleverer novels, and novels
where the ills of life have had more pathetic
expression. But by its poetic force and its

conquering spirit over those whom it touches at all, it contains the finest of his work.

In 'The Trumpet Major' you descend to a cooler air. Tragedy keeps off, or you see but a gentle shadow of it as John vanishes into the darkness, a smile on his lips and a tear in his eye for sweet Anne Garland. Virtue, in the shape of as fine a hero of chivalry as ever sat at the Table Round, is not rewarded; but that is too much of a commonplace to make a moan over, and the tone of the story is as clear and ringing as the notes from John's own trumpet. Love is still the lord of all, and a most arbitrary, inconsequent lord, too, with whom it's no use arguing, to whom it's no use showing certificates of character, or records of service. And really, when he favours Bob Loveday, who has a word to say against him? That half-suppressed fun and that rare humour of the eyes that Mr. Hardy reveals every now and again, with lapses into grimness, from 'Under the

Greenwood Tree' to 'A Few Crusted Characters,' play round every scene and character in this book, in a kindly mocking commentary, in satire without a sting.

In this, as in the shorter stories where another age is pictured, there is no insistence on detail by way of proving historical acquaintance with the epoch; but the stirring days when Boney was nightly expected to land his army on our coast in flat-bottomed boats, and rustics drilled with pikes and hurdle-sticks and cabbage-stumps on the Downs, are present to our eyes and ears. Unintentionally, and therefore the more vividly, it is an unforgetable page in history. Of all the groups in the novels, the mill folks, the kindly miller, the inconsequent Mrs. Garland, maidy Anne, John and Bob, are those we are on most familiar terms with. They are our veritable neighbours; we have none in our street or parish we know better.

'The Trumpet Major' is the tersest of the

longer stories, the fullest of nervous vigour, the most literary. The reviewer Knight in 'A Pair of Blue Eyes,' says: 'It requires a 'talented omission of your real thoughts to 'make a novel popular.' Whether that be so or not, it requires some such omission to make a novel a perfect work of art, in the narrower sense of the term. A novelist in a personal mood, confessing himself to the world, or evangelising it, may be fulfilling the greatest in him; but full revelation of emotion and opinion tends to diffuseness, and to the ups and downs of style and arrangement coincident with the swell and the exhaustion of the emotions expressed. It is not, therefore, in 'Tess' that Mr. Hardy shows himself most of a practised and perfect craftsman, but in the stories revealing fewer layers of his mind, and made of material to be more coolly dealt with, in 'Under the Greenwood Tree,' in some of the shorter stories, and especially in 'The Trumpet Major.'

If Mr. Hardy's progress were to be traced weather-chartwise, here would occur a great depression. The next two novels are inferior to the rest of his work, and one of them only in a passage or two recalls the writer's real powers. Dulness is the last quality to be associated with Mr. Hardy; but 'A Laodicean' is dull. It begins excellently, and the episode of the baptism in the Methodist chapel, where the courage of the lady of the manor is not equal to the strain put upon it by devotion to her pious father's memory, is piquant and full of promise. But Paula, the least charming of all the vacillating heroines, is forcible enough to give tone to the book; and the central fact about her being her sense of the precariousness of her social position as *parvenue* lady of the manor, the tone is one of extreme rigidity. As worldly as Ethelberta, she has none of Ethelberta's fire and dash, nor the excuse of her desperate fortunes. A Wessex and a society novel, it has the excellencies

D

of neither.   The tortuous love-story is not
very interesting ; De Stancy is an unwholesome bore ; the constant click of the excitable telegraph and the chase of the lovers,
all at cross purposes, across the Continent,
grow wearisome.   Yet there is good and
close work in it : indeed, it has the appearance of having been written in an industri-
ous fit of unowned exhaustion.   And it
could not be Mr. Hardy's without being
redeemed in some way from mere commonplace.   It has an interesting side, this 'Story
of To-day.'   The substitution of modern
energy and brains, expressed in money, for
the old feudal prestige, is the idea at the
bottom of it.   Brains and wealth have conquered.   The engineer takes possession of
the De Stancy castle and lands, and be-
queathes them to his daughter.   Not only
is there a De Stancy ready to love her with
a fierce devotion and to give her the only
thing she lacks ; but the very castle has a
personality.   It saps her modern faith, and

rouses longings in her for that old romance that money cannot buy. His own castle walls, no longer his, fight on De Stancy's side : the De Stancy ghosts are the real rivals in her heart to Somerset's claims. Indeed, so strong is this that the walls have to be burnt to the ground before you are fully assured of her loyalty to the architect hero. The castle is the most interesting character in the book.

Not much above ' A Laodicean ' in general excellence, and of slighter build, 'Two on a Tower' has at least a charm which the other lacks. The situation is somewhat morbidly unreal, but it provides a few excellent situations. Besides, the characters —they are few—draw out one's sympathies more than do the frigid ones of the preceding book. Lady Constantine and Swithin are not rustics, but their isolation and peculiar temperaments have stripped them of conventionality. The lonely woman suffering from neglect and the cruel restrictions forced on her life, feeding on her own heart till she falls in love with the much younger Swithin, whose emotions are of the most rudimentary kind, and whose intellectual interests are of the most absorbing, is the victim of one of those ironical situations in which life delights, according to the observation of Mr. Hardy. The plot is ingenious : the personages are extricated. from, or entangled in, the situations of difficulty with fine skill ; and if the book is, on the whole, thin and disappointing, and if there are few or no great passages, there is, at least, Swithin. Never has science, notoriously the most disinterested of human pursuits, been so attractively personified as in the beautiful young astronomer. Rarely has its cool, clear temper, its truthful spirit, and its limitations of sympathy, had a keener-sighted presentment.

The line of progress which had run down, now shoots up again with rapid decision in the novel published four years later than

'Two on a Tower,' 'The Mayor of Casterbridge.' With less of terse vigour than
'The Trumpet Major,' and one or two
characters, Lucetta and Farfrae, shaky in
their reality, it is yet strong in human interest, dramatic in its incidents, and in the
rise and progress of its action. No unreality
clings round the Mayor, who is as living to
us as if we had been browbeaten by him, or
been the recipients of his large capricious
favours. In this story of 'the life and
death of a man of character,' the central
figure dwarfs, with intention, the rest of the
personages, and to some extent the events,
not from any inhabitual slightness of the
incidents, or from weakness in the characters
in general. Henchard was made by nature
to be the principal feature and obstacle in
his own and his neighbour's views, and his
biographer expresses the fact. He plays the
overmastering part, tempered by human
fragility and instability, that the heath does
in 'The Return of the Native' and the

woods in 'The Woodlanders,' a part that
Mr. Hardy rarely assigns to his human personages. His personality so affects the
course and complexion of the story as to
make its construction worth the closest examination. His contradictory emotions, his
savagery and sentiment, each have their
harmonic counterparts in the incidents :
the lurid ones, like the selling of the wife at
Weydon Priors and the skimmity-ride, standing out strong against the lonely death of
the Mayor, and the quiet walk and conduct
of the still-natured Elizabeth-Jane.

'The Woodlanders' must be placed just
after Mr. Hardy's greater novels, 'Far from
the Madding Crowd,' 'The Return of the
Native,' 'The Trumpet Major,' 'The Mayor
of Casterbridge,' and 'Tess.' In all his
best work there is something recognisable
beyond the story, a poetic idea or intention of which the narrative serves as illustration and commentary. The idea or intention never fails in greatness, but sometimes

the illustration halts, and this is truer of 'The Woodlanders' than of 'The Return of the Native.' For its description of country life, and for its central conception—which may be interpreted as the effect of the woodlands on their own children, refining by their isolation and beauty Giles and Marty, and on aliens, driving Felice to revolt and selfish passion—the book deserves a high place. But Grace's story comes as a weaker note. There is something in her earlier character, at least, that does not answer to Mr. Hardy's touch. He is in fuller sympathy with less conventional, more passionate, more vivacious natures. The taint of fineladyism is about her and her story: and gentle satire would have been the most effective treatment for her troubles, arising out of the differences between her home-surroundings and her education. Such little difficulties, made so much of in life, give a novelist his chance of teaching a sense of proportion. Fitzpiers, too, is not one of his

author's happy presentations of intellectual
men.   He talks more insufferably than he
acts.   The quiet of the woods rouses despair
and revolt in Felice : it only breeds conceit
in the doctor.   In spite of weaknesses, the
book claims our sympathies strongly in other
directions, and many of its descriptive passages, Midsummer Eve in the woods, for
instance, Sherton in the cider season, the
barking of the trees, the view from Rubdon
Hill over the blue apple valley, are of a kind
to cling to the memory as do only a few
of the scenes that have met our bodily eyes.

'Tess' has been pushed to the front
because of the problems it deals with, but
perhaps the place assigned to it is the right
one, for, judged by the strength of its appeal
to human sympathies, it is doubtless his
greatest book.   'Sent out in all sincerity
' of purpose,' its author said of it in his first
preface, but sincerity seems hardly to express
the intense and burning earnestness with
which his championship of Tess is filled.

This very earnestness has shaken his hand
now and again, and prevented an idyll of
singular beauty, a tragedy of force enough
to drive complacency out of the smuggest,
from being a complete artistic success. Its
greatness is proved by its lovers mostly for-
getting its defects in their memory of the
whole. Only in summoning a judicial mood
do they call to mind that there are impro-
babilities in the story—and Angel's proposal
to Izz to go with him to Brazil is not a slight
one ; why, if he wished to 'rule his future
domesticities himself, instead of kissing the
pedagogic rod of convention,' didn't he go
and fetch Tess? Then the drivelling John
Durbeyfield drivels a little too much, and
Tess and Angel talk too big. Very likely a
definitive edition of the book is wanted.' It
may be a matter of question whether the
murder, or the madness its cause, or the
hanging its consequence, be strictly necessary. It is a book that holds both cheeks
ready for the smiting of the little critic, as

do not a few of the great books of the world,
till tradition has raised a fence of reverence
about them, and they become fetishes. But,
in no carping mood, one must own that, apart
from the central figure, it is poorer than any
of the other great novels in strong presentations of character, as it is richer, or, at least
subtler, in its interpretation of Nature.

Mr. Hardy meant the book to be a battle-
ground, and it has been so. Had he merely
appealed to sentiment, omitted the violent
acts of the end, and made claims for Tess's
loveableness, not for her virtue, he might
have carried all his readers with him. Many
would have been tender-hearted enough to
be sorry for Tess, who treat her author's
insistence on her purity either as an outrage
or a quibble. He preferred to make war.
The omission of the murder and its consequences would have left the problem
stated, certainly, of the woman undergoing
her undue share of suffering; but Mr. Hardy
does not feel his business stop at the state-

ment of problems. He gives their working-out in individual lives. First he shows Tess as grievously wronged, and then how such wrong may be, by the meekest natures, thrown back with awful violence in the world's face, a fact worth exemplifying at the cost of readers' feelings.

The chief cause of offence besides the sub-title ' A Pure Woman,' or rather because of the sub-title, is Tess's return to D'Urberville. It has been said to be improbable. It has also been said to prove her impurity. Surely here Mr. Hardy was pointing to one of the great facts of life which ethics are bound to face, a fact neither moral nor immoral, that the human will has limits of vitality, which means limits of resistance, that, only let the struggle be terrible enough for any individual, he will give in. The power of resistance varies infinitely in weak and strong, but so does the strength of the attack ; and a sensitive nature has less chance of victory than a stolid one. The

surrender—in the virtuous chiefly physical—
may mean, in fortunate cases, death, but it
may mean, unless suicide be resorted to, a
continuance of exhausted life, in which circumstances easily win. And saints are
subject in like manner, if not in like degree,
as sinners, to this law of human limitation,
which is as inevitable as the coming on of
old age, and has its examples beyond what
are known as the temptations of life. Every
man who has given up, for weariness, the
ideals of his youth, has experienced this
mastery of the spirit by the weakness of
the body. The surrender took place, it is
said, because Tess was pagan, and so the
miracle could not happen. But does the
miracle give more than the utmost of one's
own strength sublimated by imagination or
faith? Fatigue is not a condonation lightly
to be put forward for weakness, but it is a
cogent plea in that final court of appeal to
which only the great suits and struggles of
life are carried. Tess presents the type
of woman for generations dear to her con-

demners, ready to merge her whole being in another's, in perfect devotion and trust. The other miserably failed her. Angel's shoddy idealism stuck at one fact, and ignored all the rest of his knowledge of her. There was nothing else in life, and the brothers and sisters prevented death from being an alternative : her domestic affections combined with exhaustion and completed the surrender, such as it was. Then Angel came back—proof she had been lied to. The world returned, but with it the streak of madness in her blood awoke, and she had revenge on what had cursed her life.

Condonation or explanation of this kind does not mean the substitution of an easier code. Mr. Hardy has, inferentially, adopted a harder one and a higher one than the world is likely to reach for some time, namely, that the measure of purity, and of the reverse, is in the heart's intentions and desires. His thesis is that Tess's desires were pure : so, therefore, was she. In estimating the morality of his point of view, it may not be unhelpful to read, by way of contrast, the words of a reviewer in a well-considered organ of literary opinion. 'Angel Clare is a good man, just and not unduly severe. It is natural that he should discard his wife, not unnatural, considering her sensual attractions, that he should come back to her, and not notice the lemon-coloured finery.' Even his hardest critics—save only this one —will recognise here a depth to which he has not sunk.

Whether he has proved his case or not, he has, with more courage and chivalry than any other, thrown down his glove in defence of the woman who, be she good or bad, in the particular catastrophe, always pays the whole penalty of suffering and disgrace. He has tilted hard against conventions and the timid silences, and he has made himself be listened to. It is not pity he asks for Tess. Philanthropy has long pitied her. He would draw her 'poor wounded name' from obloquy, and raise her to the level where the innocency of her intentions gives her a right to dwell. But if he claims justice rather than pity, he bestows pity on her abundantly himself, and on Tess, more than on any other of his creations, has he poured out his humanity.

A word as to the shorter stories, dealt with elsewhere. 'Wessex Tales,' a collection of five, contributed to various periodicals from 1879 to 1888, and published in the latter year, includes some work at his best level, 'The Three Strangers,' since successfully dramatised, 'The Distracted Preacher,' and 'The Withered Arm.' The two others, 'Interlopers at the Knap' and 'Fellow Townsmen,' in greyer tones and minor key, contain some subtle reading of motive and character. 'A Group of Noble Dames,' published in 1891, is a collection of piquant stories made out of some family legends of his county. A storm-bound Field and Antiquarian Club, being unable to visit, as they had planned, the antiquities of the neighbourhood, the local historian tells the tale of 'The First Countess of Wessex,' as a substitute for 'the regulation papers on 'deformed butterflies, fossil ox-horns, pre-'historic dung-mixens, and such like, that 'usually occupied the more serious attention 'of the members.' His example is followed, and the comments of the members contribute not a little to the abundant humour which is a feature of the stories, notwithstanding the fact that only two out of the ten can be classed as comedy. The conversational style in which they are told keeps the atmosphere cool, and gives opportunity for that light mocking tone which Mr. Hardy can adopt with much skill when he would show the humour of serious situations, and which, being neither bitter nor hilarious, has no incongruity in tales of sadness. 'Life's Little Ironies'—published in March 1894—consists of stories contributed to magazines from 1882 to 1893. 'A Tradition 'of Eighteen Hundred and Four' which is hardly an 'Irony,' and the bubbling fun of 'A Few Crusted Characters,' the second part of the book, mitigate the gloom of the rest, which is of every complexion of sorrow, 'The Son's Veto,' and 'For Conscience Sake' being of the subdued order of 'Fellow Townsmen,' while 'A Tragedy of Two Ambitions' and 'To Please his Wife' have more of unrestrained bitterness about them. 'On the Western Circuit' and 'The Fiddler of the Reels,' two powerful studies of morbid mental and moral conditions, have been followed by another in the same strain, 'An Imaginative Woman,' not yet included in a volume.

Since 'The Pursuit of the Well-Beloved : A Sketch of a Temperament,' which appeared as a serial in *The Illustrated London News* in 1892, has not yet been published in book form, perhaps we may hope the ending given to the story is not the inevitable one. The weary Jocelyn, tossed to and fro all his life by his homeless emotions, might surely at last find the rest he sought beneath the waves, and not be picked up only to meet a ghastly reminder of one of his many failures to

E

realise his dream. The fickle hero, a sculptor,
is constancy itself to one never-fading vision
in his mind.   In his search for its realisation
he loves here, there, and everywhere, but the
vision flees at the approach of the earthly
beloved, and he will make no compromise.
Late in life he finds his ideal bound fast in
the grandchild of one of his early temporary
loves; but his tardy faithfulness is unrewarded, for his young wife, his beloved,
has her own vision, which is not a picture of
himself.   His conduct in the circumstances
is of a generosity the law would frown on.
' The Pursuit of the Well-Beloved ' is full of
Mr. Hardy's peculiar sympathy with complexities of the soul, and his pity is not ill-
spent on the hero, who was no professional
breaker of hearts.   The roll of his loves has
yet something of the comic about it: a
shorter one had amply served as manifestation of his temperament.   But the ugliness
that might lurk in such a story is killed by
the conviction forced on us of the reality of
Jocelyn's ideal.

STORYWRIGHT

IV

STORYWRIGHT

OF all Mr. Hardy's gifts, that of making pictures occurs most readily to one's mind at the mention of his name, though in the conception of some characters, and in the ideas at the back of some stories, he has revealed a higher imaginative power. His invention of incidents—both those of the character-revealing order and those that flash on the vision, delights of colour and grouping, complete in themselves—is of the readiest and the most inexhaustible. Nearly all his situations give the idea of actually having been seen rather than having been thought out by their inventor; our sight of them is the more vivid. This special talent generally urges its possessor to writing novels of the heroic sword-and-cloak order, but Mr. Hardy has used it mostly for lighting up the life of modern days. His colouring is bold, his detail precise, and grouped with conscious art; his high lights are emphasised. It is through this emphasis, by which he sometimes attacks rather than persuades the eyes, that he now and again goes wrong. The commonplace in incident has not often ·satisfied him; he loves to drag his personages into bizarre situations, where they grow desperate or light-headed, where circumstances stand to them in strong contrast, mark their isolation, prove their weakness or their strength. In the sequestered vale of Wessex life it is as often the struggles and catastrophes he has presented as the even tenor of rustic ways.

His plans of structure in his stories are various, but a plan there always is; there are no stray disjointed sketches. 'Under

the Greenwood Tree,' 'The Trumpet Major,
and 'The Woodlanders' are not built on a
dramatic plan, but they have complete pictorial unity. In 'Desperate Remedies,' and
'Far from the Madding Crowd,' of much
more elaborate mechanism, the separate
parts fit in with rare precision. The three
tragedies, 'The Mayor of Casterbridge,' 'The
Return of the Native,' and 'Tess' are of the
traditional five act build. It would be easy
to divide the first into the stages of a regular
drama : Act I.—The sale of the wife at
Weydon Priors Fair, Henchard's remorse
and his vow. Act II.—The prosperity con-
sequent on his keeping the vow, and on his
strenuous ambitions and endeavours, eccen-
tricity and weakness, nevertheless, creeping
in and paving the way for his troubles in
Act III., where Farfrae outrivals him in love
and business, the rivalry provoking the worst
in the mayor's character, and bringing on
the days of adversity and degradation in
Act IV. There, having drunk misery to the

lees, the good in him comes to the surface under the companionship of that still soul Elizabeth-Jane, his chastened happiness, nevertheless, preparing the further wretchedness in the last act, when Newson returns to steal her affections from him, and when, bereft of love and hope and fortune, he shoulders his workman's tools again, wanders in a circle round and round the spot where his heart still lives, till, wearied out, he lies down in his old servant's hut in Egdon to die.

But Mr. Hardy's chief narrative talent does not lie in the integral structure of his stories; but, as has been said, in his rich invention of incident. A host of others will suggest themselves if but a few of those events be named that test character, or are clad in circumstance dramatically and poetically appropriate. Manston watching the fire where his wife is supposed to have been burnt; the rival lovers, Dick and Shinar, at the honey-taking; Oak's prowess at the sheep-shearing, his lady looking on; the

dulcet piping of his flute to Bathsheba's
song, 'the shearers reclining against each
'other as at suppers in the early ages of the
'world'; the troopers riding into the stream
by Overcombe mill, and catching the miller's
cherries in their forage-caps ; the hangman
singing to the listening cottagers, while the
condemned man sitting in the chimney-
corner joins in the ghastly chorus; Rhoda
united again to Farmer Lodge over the
strangled body of their son, his wife a
stranger standing apart; Henchard's sale
of his wife at the fair; the death of Giles
in One Chimney Hut—Grace, for whom he
died, on one side, and proud to be there,
her erring husband on the other, too peni-
tent for his own misdeeds to question her
conduct; Joshua clutching Cornelius's arm
in the moment of hesitation that sent their
worthless father to his death in the weir;
Tess baptising her child Sorrow, with the '
audience of sleepy, awe-struck children
about her; the homeless Durbeyfield family

setting up their *ménage* over the vault of
their noble ancestors in Kingsbere—a list like
this could be multiplied many times; only
it could not illustrate the rare genius shown
in the revealing and commenting circumstances. This, his strongest faculty as a
story-teller, points to the fact further exem-
plified by his style, that he is a writer not
of even perfection but of great passages and
great moments. But his moments have
occasional power to give the tone to a whole
book. One can pick out cases where the
incidents are sensational, or too elaborately
furnished with picturesque detail, where they
overstep the limits of artistic propriety in
their determination to besiege the senses
and sensibilities. The policemen closing
in round Tess at Stonehenge is the type of
this offending. But such offences are the
defects of a great quality.

In short stories, made up of distinct incidents, as distinguished from sketches, scenes,
glimpses and phases of character, Mr. Hardy

is the master, in England, at least. His
triumphs in structure are there. It is not
only that he has learnt not to be discursive,
where order, clearness, deftness, are the first
qualities, where fine cut and finish tell more
than wealth of material. His scheme, conscious or unconscious, has affected his choice
of subject, his style, and his tone. Some of
the plots of his shorter tales might, of course,
have been elaborated into novels, but a
further elaboration does not pressingly suggest itself. As you look, you feel that a
small canvas is the more fitting. He has
seen that the chief use of short stories is to
skim the surface of life, and when he has
struck a tragic note in these, he has re-
strained the expression as far as possible.
What is food for light satire or laughter, and
incidents that draw a sigh rather than a wail,
are the materials he moulds best and most
frequently into this form. His style is in-
separably knit in with the lightness, aptness,
and fine proportions of the structure, and

neither in style nor structure has he reached
a higher level of craftsmanship than in 'A
Group of Noble Dames.'

Mr. Hardy's invention is more, not less,
appreciated, if you know something of how
he seeks his plots. Many have doubtless
been born in his own brain, and the light
that reveals the meaning of the story and
gives it life, is from his own imagination;
but of Wessex history, as well as Wessex
landscape, he has made skilful use. The
incidents, memories, and traditions that have
given him suggestions, he has probably heard
by word of mouth. Legends of Boney's
projected invasion, for instance, lie thick
about the Wessex Downs, for Lulworth Cove
was to be the landing-place, or actually was
so, according to 'A Tradition of Eighteen
Hundred and Four,' and tales told him as a
boy lived vividly in his memory till he made
them into 'The Trumpet Major.' But the
dry bones of some that he has quickened
into life an interested reader can find if he

takes the trouble to forage in county records. The story of Pa'son Billy Toogood's forgetfulness in 'A Few Crusted Characters,' for instance, is a familiar one to Dorset folks, his original being a famous old rector of Frampton, the Rev. William Butler, friend of the Prince Regent, and notorious and untirable fox-hunter.

The incidents in the story of 'Tess' are doubtless in the main purely imaginary. They are built, however, on a structure of suggestive facts, namely, on the history of the famous house of Turberville, and the existence, in large numbers, among the Dorsetshire peasantry at the present day, of the descendants of many noble and powerful feudal houses, since early in the last century great alterations having taken place in the ownership of land. The Turbervilles descend from Sir Pagan or Sir Payne, a follower of the Conqueror, whose name appears in Battle Abbey Roll. About Henry III.'s time they became possessed of the manor of Bere,

where they resided for five hundred years.
The site of the old house can still be seen
at a farm called The Court, below Woodbury
Hill. The county history contains a picture
of it. In the Turberville aisle, in the fine old
church that stands just above, are the family
vaults and the tombs: 'canopied, altar-
' shaped, and plain ; their carvings being
' defaced and broken ; their brasses torn
' from the matrices, the rivet-holes remain-
' ing like marten-holes in a sand-cliff,' is the
accurate description in 'Tess,' of the present
state of the latter. On the 'beautifully
' traceried window of many lights' occur the
names of numerous Turbervilles, with their
arms : Ermine, a lion rampant, crowned
gules. Crest, a castle argent—' a ramping
' lion, and a castle over him,' is Tess's version, her heraldic information being derived
from the old silver spoon that stirred the
family soup. A younger branch of the once
powerful house settled in Wool (Wellbridge)
in Elizabeth's time. The present house,

probably rebuilt by Sir John Turberville,
Sheriff of Dorset in 1652, is the scene of
Tess's confession to Angel. The pictures of
the gruesome ladies that frightened Angel
with their hideous distortion of his wife's
features, can be seen on the staircase still.
Out of these facts, then, the debasement of
noble names and the strain of noble blood
in the Dorsetshire peasantry, superadded to
a desire to do battle against an old injustice,
and make a chivalrous defence, has sprung
the story of 'Tess.'

Again, from a little bit of pedigree that
would to most suggest a mere comment, were
they to examine its dates, has grown the
best of all the stories in the 'Noble Dames.'
It tells how Thomas Horner of Mells married Susanna Strangways of Melbury, and
that Elizabeth, their daughter, born in 1723,
married Stephen Fox (afterwards Lord Il-
chester) in 1736, that is, at thirteen. The
shocked comment of an ordinary reader is
turned into the story of Betty Dornell, first

Countess of Wessex, in which the subtle play of motive, circumstance, and character, owe just nothing at all to the original fact, and yet seem its inevitable outcome. The gruesome tale of ' Barbara of the House of Grebe ' has grown out of some family chronicles, vivified beyond recognition by Mr. Hardy's fertile imagination. Chene Manor, Barbara's home, is Canford Magna, which in the middle and till the end of last century was the house of Sir John Webb. His only surviving daughter Barbara married the fifth Earl of Shaftesbury, but whether the character of that nobleman deserved commemoration as Lord Uplandtowers, my dry-as-dust chronicles do not reveal. Barbara's death at Florence, the survival of but one child out of eleven, can be seen in family pedigrees, but of her marriage with Willowes, and all that makes the interest of the ghastly tale, there is not a trace.

The scene of ' Anne, Lady Baxby,' is Sherborne (Sherton) Castle. Held by George,

second Earl of Bristol, and his son, Lord
Digby, for the king, it was besieged by Lord
Bedford, leader of the Parliamentary forces,
and Lady Digby's brother. The clash of
family feeling and politics, and the commu-
nication between the brother and sister pro-
vided a slight framework, but the humour of
the tale is Mr. Hardy's own.

The original of the Eighth Dame was
Penelope, daughter and heiress of Mary,
Countess of Rivers. The three lovers were
Sir John Gage of Firle, Sir William Hervey
of Ickworth, and Sir George Trenchard of
Wolveton. Her threat of displeasure should
they quarrel with each other on her account,
her playful promise to marry all of them in
turn, and her fulfilment of the promise, are
authenticated traditions, out of which has
sprung the strange and melancholy story.

The only interest of bringing such hard
dry facts as these into the country of
romance, is in their further illustration of the
way in which Mr. Hardy's imagination works.

F

The method of many a poet and novelist is first to catch a motive for poem or story, which may be a native of anywhere under the sun, and then to clothe it in a garment of home manufacture. Mr. Hardy generally works the contrary way. For some of his characters, but in a much greater degree for his plots, incidents, and scenes, he has dug in the soil he knows best, using the material ready to his hand. The foundation made of this, he has let his imagination play freely about the superstructure, but the material of the base, and the character of the surroundings, have generally reminded him of his obligations to congruity, and kept his imagination in fitting moods. This may seem to be less the case with his personages, but his study of men and women has taught him how subtle a thing is human nature, and how continually it is slipping the bonds of local and racial harness. Wessex, and Mayfair, and the warm South, have each special backgrounds for their dramas, each their own speech, each their traditions of translating thoughts and motives into action ; but at the back of the several local manifestations, the general human instincts, impulses, and peculiarities, find kindred thousands of leagues apart.

MEN AND WOMEN

V

MEN AND WOMEN

OF characters in novels that are characters
at all, and not shadows, there are first those
we actually live with. Dr. Primrose, Toby
Shandy, Dugald Dalgetty, D'Artagnan, Beatrix
Esmond, and Jane Eyre, are of the company. Probability has just as much and as
little to do with the fact of their existence
as it would have in real life. Then there
are those whose features, temperaments,
attitudes, we remember long, but as we
remember the great portraits in a gallery.
They have much to tell, only they do not
come out of their frames to tell it. Characters they are ; but hardly personages, and

they gain admiration rather than wide acquaintance.

Of Mr. Hardy's creations a number belong certainly to the first class. Dick Dewy, Fancy, Henchard, Bathsheba, Bob Loveday, Tony, Lizzie Newberry, Betty Dornell, and Tess, are all warm with life. They live in a good many people's world already: they would live in a wider world were there more comfortable complacency in the Wessex novels: the lack of it is a real grievance to the ordinary novel reader.

Mr. Hardy uses the two methods of character presentation, and each with care. His analyses are minute, fine-drawn, and frequent, but they nearly always tally with actions, and if his commentaries are interesting they are never strictly necessary. With his ready invention of incident, he is rarely at a loss for testing and revealing scenes. Nevertheless, a good many of his personages must be given over to the portrait class, Edward Springrove, for instance, and, in fact, all the admirably conducted young architect heroes, along with most of the conventional London folks. Elfrida's step-mother, an ambitious attempt, is incoherent. Perhaps one's desire mingles with, and in-fluences, a conviction that Knight and Paula never lived. Tamsin and Lucetta are shadowy ; John Durbeyfield is improbable enough to make one believe him to have been drawn straight from life. Farfrae, though particularly shrewd observation went to his making, is rather an unconventional theory on two legs than a live Scot.

His greatest successes have lain with subtle characters, and with such as are apt to be readily stirred by the winds of impulse and caprice, even though one has to put aside Giles, and the Trumpet Major, Marty South, and Oak, to make the generalisation. The other characteristics, or circumstances of character, that he loves to bring into play, are passion — so much stronger a reality with him than with most English

novelists — powers of fascination, mental
gifts—here he treads on dangerous ground,
for the greatly endowed in this direction
generally prove strutting coxcombs in novels
—and rebellion against alien surroundings.

The comic rustics are his most popu-
larly known characters. There are the
simple ones, too unsophisticated to do anything but show their simplicity, and be a
perpetual and involuntary comedy ; and
their neighbours, the witty ones, who have
mostly a spice of wickedness about them.
The timid man is a stock character, but he
is repeated with a difference. Leaf in a
kindly innocent way enjoys the social dis-
tinction of never having ' had no head.'
' He's very clever for a silly chap, good-
' now, sir. You never knowed a young feller
' keep his smock-frocks so clane,' is grateful praise to his heart. Poorgrass has the
timidity mingled with a good deal of head
and vanity, and a dash of malice. ' " Heh-
' heh ! well, I wish to noise nothing abroad

'—nothing at all!" murmured Poorgrass,
' diffidently. " But we are born to things—
' that's true. Yet I would rather my trifle
' were hid; though, perhaps, a high nature
' is a little high, and at my birth all things
' were possible to my Maker, and he may
' have begrudged no gifts. . . . But under
' your bushel, Joseph! under your bushel
' with you ! " ' Christian Cantle, the ' man
' of mournfullest make,' is more of Leaf's
shape, save that he wants Leaf's joyous
complacency. They are various in gait and
utterance when you begin to run over the
group that includes Grandfer Cantle, the
' playward' old man; the stammering Randle
—' " 'a can cuss, mem, as well as you or I,
' but 'a can't speak a common speech to
' save his life";' Coggan, who, with all re-
spect for the intellect and fervour of Dis-
senters, hated 'a feller who'd change his old
' ancient doctrine for the sake of getting to
' heaven'; that resourceful sergeant of the
Overcombe recruits—' " What's that man

' a-saying of in the rear rank?" "Please,
' sir, 'tis Anthony Cripplestraw, wanting to
' know how he's to bite off his katridge,
' when he haven't a tooth left in 's head?"
' "Man! why, what's your genius for war?
' Hold it up to your right-hand man's
' mouth, to be sure, and let him nip it off
' for ye";' the maltster with his grievance
against all who should dispute his age or
put in claims for the venerableness of others
—'"Ye be no old man worth naming—
' no old man at all. Yer teeth baint half
' gone yet; and what's a old man's standing
' if so be his teeth baint gone? . . . 'Tis a
' poor thing to be sixty, when there's people
' far past four score—a boast weak as water";'
and Worm with his depressing formula, ' " I
' be a poor wambling man, and life's a mere
' bubble." '

But Mr. Hardy's comic rustics, as they
are the most generally appreciated of his
personages, so also have they been most
abused, for their simplicity, but still more

for their wit. The language they, and the other characters, too, use, and the ideas they express, have been called quite impossible for the 'illiterate clods whom he de-' scribes.' Here the typical townsman speaks. Mr. Hardy never attempts to describe 'clods,' and illiterateness is compatible not only with mental endowments but with a wide and even an ambitious vocabulary. The Dorset labourer is an articulate person, and he is proverbially aspiring in his language—his very malaprops are a sign of it. Mr. Hardy has claimed for the Wessex peasants kinship with the Warwickshire breed that delighted Shakespeare. Seeing the affinity between those he had himself watched and listened to, and the dramatist's witty clowns and humorous simpletons, he dug in his own soil with the more zest, and brought up native material. But the consciousness of the kinship had doubtless considerable influence on the manner in which he presented them, and they may speak with more of an Elizabethan Warwickshire accent than strict realism would admit of. The objection raises an important and interesting question in fiction. In the delineation of character and the selection of incident the novelist is free as the poet and dramatist to extract the essence, to sublimate, to arrange. But in the record of conversation a strenuous attempt has been made of late years to force him to bring the phonograph into use, and to demand the actual finite words and not the final sense. The breach or observance of this rule is a favourite test of common-place critics, for the mimicry of speech and accent, one of the most ordinary of accomplishments, has a knowing air about it. Literalism in such matters is not quite possible : for human speech is often too elliptical, too stammering, to be intelligible without the aid of the intonations, gestures, and expressions which cannot utter themselves in print. But an approximation to it

is, of course, convenient, inasmuch as it
enhances the verisimilitude of the scene and
dialogue to literal readers ; and in depicting
the more superficial or the more commonplace events of life it is an appropriate
method.   However, the rule of transcribing
literally Mr. Hardy has never attempted to
keep.   Half his offence—if offence it be—is
not due to unskilful reporting, but to his
deliberately using a poetical rather than a
phonographic method.   He has defended
himself on the point of his lack of literalness
in the transcription of dialect forms, by
declaring such literalness 'disturbs the
' proper balance of a true representation by
' unduly insisting upon the grotesque ele-
' ment; thus directing attention to a point
' of inferior interest, and diverting it from
' the speaker's meaning, which is by far the
' chief concern where the aim is to depict
' the men and their natures rather than
' their dialect forms.'[1]   These words are
applicable here, if we widen ' dialect forms '

[1] *Athenæum*, Nov. 30, 1878.

to include all that concerns the speech and
powers of expression of the Dorset peasants.
The meaning to be conveyed is that the
peasants are all unlearned in town ways, yet
quick-witted, humorous, full of grotesque
and unexpected ideas, with a fine language
on their lips, got partly from the Bible, perhaps, and partly from their fathers' bequests
of an older tongue. But listening to them,
a stranger could hardly pierce their speech
enough to find all this out; so Mr. Hardy,
knowing them, and estimating his readers'
capacities and limitations, attempts a translation of the spirit instead of abiding by
the letter. He is not consistent in this
of course; some of the wit and happy
blundering have come straight from life,
doubtless; and his translation may now and
again end in not very fine-pointed caricature. Yet in his main method he exer-
cises a right that fiction can least of all
dispense with now that its purposes are
growing more and more enlarged. Only,

after asserting this right, it strikes one as a little absurd to give Coggan and Poorgrass, and Penny and Spinks, the reception of argument : better, surely, first to be grateful for the fun they afford to a dull world, and then to go and learn firsthand something of country minds and manners.

Besides the comic characters, there are others, strongly marked, finely shaded, representing the dignity, the intelligence, and the sturdiness of rustic life. Of these are Tranter Dewy, the kindly cynic, the genial and affectionate Miller Loveday, the elder Springrove, the 'poet with a rough skin,' Oak, type of the patient love 'which many ' waters cannot quench, nor the floods ' drown,' the pure-natured Winterborne, friend of all that grew in the woods, and the trusty and resourceful reddleman.

Mr. Hardy's villains are mostly of one type, hot-blooded and wild-blooded, their senses the strongest thing in their nature. But the only sensualist, pure and simple, is

G

D'Urberville ; the others have some mental
endowment, or special personal charm to
aid them in their fascination, if not as a
saving grace. Manston is a man of parts ;
he has not run all to brutality. Troy's
romance is tawdry sentimentalism, but his
fascination of bodily skill, impudent talk and
assurance, is real enough. Wildeve has
grace of movement, delicacy of manner, and
sometimes of perception. Even Festus
Derriman, braggart and buffoon, has his
vanity stirred by a lively imagination. There
is an attractive air of magnificence and
romance about him, till he is found out.
Fitzpiers, too, also on the borders of villain-
dom, is carried away as much by intellectual
temptations as by sensual, and the fineness
of some of his fibres he shows in his fair and
generous-minded bargain with Grace. They
are mainly, in short, types of the temptations
of quick-natured and warm-natured men.
Dare stands apart from these, a cold-blooded
imp, ready for any meanness or trickery,

and nearer him perhaps is Mop Ollamoor, for he is too irresponsible to be grouped with the passionate ones, this ' deil that ' came fiddlin' thro' the toun,' and bound the hysterical spirit of Car'line in dancing captivity.

Mr. Barrie tells that in a library copy of one of the ' Wessex Novels ' was found written in a lady's handwriting, ' Oh, how I *hate* Thomas Hardy ! ' Every woman will go straight to the point where the novelist has offended this sensitive and emphatic reader, whether she shares the sentiment or not. The offence is that Bathsheba, Fancy, Elfride, and sweet Anne Garland are fickle and wayward, they play the fool and put themselves in the wrong over and over again, and are totally want-ing in that statuesque and goddess-like dignity that women naturally wish to have regarded as the characteristic garment of their sex. But more than that, and worse : these frail, uncertain creatures are fascinat-ing ; there is no doubt about it, each of them .

' Light and humorous in her toying,
Oft building hopes, and soon destroying,
Long, but sweet in the enjoying.'

They play havoc with readers' hearts, and cause confusion in ideals. And it is so bad for the world to be confirmed in its already too strong opinion that attractiveness and loveableness are hardly things of the proprieties or the superficial moralities. Not that caprice, by the way, is a peculiarly feminine quality in Mr. Hardy's eyes. Bob Loveday and the Mayor have it as strongly as any of the women. It is one of the fascinations of human character for him. ' Perhaps there was a proneness to inconstancy ' in her nature,' he says of Elfride, ' a nature ' to those who contemplate it from a standpoint beyond the influence of that inconstancy the most exquisite of all in its ' plasticity and ready sympathies.' In Jocelyn Pearston fickleness is an actual malady.

A critic recently advised him to try his

hand at the modern woman. May he find
strength to resist the suggestion if she be the
thing so named in recent novels ! Indeed,
what is more likely to be the real thing,
judging from manifestations in the world
rather than in fiction—an inchoate mass of
contrary tendencies, at an ungraceful stage
of growth, but only unwholesome because
unmade—is a ticklish thing for art. I do
not think modernness, save in superficial
accent, is lacking in the group that includes
Ethelberta, Ella Marchill, Lizzie Newberry,
and Eustacia. And persons and things
styled 'modern' are always merely conspicuous symptoms of tendencies which, if
they be real, may in time absorb or live along-
side, but never altogether efface, the things
and types of old growth. Bathsheba is not
of yesterday only, or to-day. Our grand-
children will know her, sigh over the frailty
of womenkind, and love her always.

Mr. Hardy has not missed the opportunity
given him by his studies in human nature of

joining in that fascinating amusement, the making of generalisations on womenkind. The usual way of playing the game is to begin by taking for granted that woman is a profound and rather unholy mystery. Then by a sleight of hand of incredible quickness, and an assurance in the voice and eyes which is more than half the trick, the conjuror turns up a queen and a knave as final solution, proves that he is a very clever fellow, that there was no mystery after all, and that the whole truth about womenkind can be summed up in a couple of epigrams. Then the game begins all over again, but always at the mystery. Mr. Hardy does not play this way exactly, but he makes frequent generalisations of which an interesting collection could be made out of the earlier books. As generalisations are always too sweeping, he has honestly bought greater scientific accuracy at the price of an occasional self-contradiction. And he has not dramatised or personified his generalisations.

His women are strongly individual. His
attitude towards them has always been that
of an indulgent critic, keen-sighted for fail-
ings, and just : he has neither idealised nor
flattered them, but he has broken a lance
not seldom for their freedom from the conventions that stunt and warp them. His
women of strong passions are portrayed with
special vividness. Miss Aldclyffe is an ex-
asperating companion : in her ravenous
hunger for affection from Cytherea there is
neither charm nor comfort ; but she has yet
a power stronger than most young and graceful heroines to stir one's sympathies. Eustacia, the 'raw material of a goddess,' her
' Pagan eyes full of nocturnal mysteries,'
who 'had mentally walked round love, told
' the towers thereof, considered its palaces,
' and concluded that love was but a doleful
' joy,' who yet ' desired it, as one in a desert
' would be thankful for brackish water,'
beating her heart out against her Egdon
prison, has that compelling force to win

sympathy from different temperaments that marks the woman made for tragedy. Felice, too, though less convincing, draws us against ourselves, as she utters her terrible consciousness of the quiet that enwraps her—'I lay 'awake all last night, and I could hear the 'scrape of snails creeping up the window 'glass.' With that one-sided remembrance we have of vivid natures we seem always to see her with that 'sort of sorrow on her face 'as if she chid her own soul.' Poor Tess is different from these. They are rebels by nature, who would exhaust their passions at an extravagant rate, and live and die with hungry hearts. Tess has the warm overflowing affection that seeks an unchanging investment in domestic life. Her madness is an accident as unforeseeable as her betrayal. Picotee, whose lines fall in happier, more sheltered circumstances, and who has a less dangerous inheritance, is her own sister.

Some there are in whom desires and passions have been starved. Elizabeth-Jane is one, that quiet-stepping but strong-natured girl, with her ' field-mouse fear of the coulter ' of destiny, a legacy from her early years of ' misery.' Another is Marty, one of the subtlest and most striking of Mr. Hardy's or anyone else's country girls. Bred in poverty, to constant work, and to more than usual solitude, she has yet that keen interest in other folks, and that bright mind that might have meant wit and brilliancy in different circumstances. Ignorant and uncouth and with a spice of mischief in her, the interest takes grotesque forms, as in the case of her interference on Grace's behalf in her letter to Fitzpiers, and her chalked-up rhyme on Giles's door. These are bye-plays in the working of her pure and steadfast nature, and in the history of her long, unregarded, unrewarded love.

One cannot summarise all the types here, but a few pictures, chosen at random from the scenes where women play a part, will present women's nature from no narrow point

of view. Let us take Bathsheba the 'shapely maid,' wiling the time away on the top of the waggon of furniture by surveying herself in the mirror: Eustacia seeking for emancipation from the gloomy heath at the hands of Clym, its product and lover; Tess happy in the return of the unconscious affection of Angel as he bears her in his sleep to Bindon, and end with Marty at the grave of Giles—
' As this solitary and silent girl stood there
' in the moonlight, a straight slim figure,
' clothed in a plaitless gown, the contours of
' womanhood so undeveloped as to be
' scarcely perceptible, the marks of poverty
' and toil effaced by the misty hour, she
' touched sublimity at points, and looked
' almost like a being who had rejected with
' indifference the attribute of sex for the
' loftier quality of abstract humanism. . . .

' " Now, my own, own love," she whispered,
' " You are mine, and on'y mine ; for she has
' forgot 'ee at last, although for her you
' died. But I—whenever I get up I'll think

' of 'ee, and whenever I lie down I 'll think
' of 'ee. Whenever I plant the young larches
' I 'll think that none can plant as you
' planted ; and whenever I split a gad, and
' whenever I turn the cider wring, I 'll say
' none could do it like you.   If ever I forget
' your name let me forget home and heaven !
' . . . But no, no, my love, I never can for-
' get 'ee ; for you was a good man, and did
' good things ! " '

Not in the case of maidens only has youth
a charm in Mr. Hardy's hands.   His boys
have not that heroic mien they would doubtless desire to appear with, for he has a
humiliating way of stripping off the outer
garment of dignity.   Indeed, it might be
said, whom he loves he laughs at.   But they
have the grace that makes them attractive
in their elders' eyes.   His prime favourites
among them, and ours—they are three, Dick
Dewy, Bob Loveday, and the never enough
appreciated young astronomer, Swithin—have
one charm more than the flighty heroines, in

that they lack the streak of worldliness hardly
ever absent from his women, especially his
women of fascination. Swithin is poorly
supported, and the tower is not so good a
background as the greenwood tree or the
open downs; but about his clear crystal
nature, his quick response to calls from the
remote heavens, and his aloofness from
ordinary human things, till he is forced into
love by the persistence of a woman older
than himself, there is a radiance of youth
and grace and the ideal. Dick, however, is
the prince of charmers. He may present
the card of Dewy and Son, Tranters and
Hauliers, as proof of his dignity, and lay in
a goodly stock of chairs and tables and
victuals and drink for his housekeeping;
nevertheless, whenever we think of him it is
as he pens the desperate letter, which left it
doubtful 'whether he there and then left off
' loving Miss Fancy Day; whether he had
' never loved her seriously, and never meant
' to; whether he had been dying up to the

' present moment, and now intended to get
' well again ; or whether he had hitherto been
' in good health, and intended to die for her
' forthwith'; or, as he gives a juvenile hop
with one foot to put himself in step with the
parson, previous to telling him of his matri-
monial projects; or, as he shouts to Enoch
across the wood, ' " D 'ye know who I
' be-e-e-e-? . . . Dick Dew-w-w-w-wy ! . . .
' Just a-ma-a-a-a-a-arried ! . . . This is my
' wife, Fa-a-a-a-a-ancy ! " (holding her up to
' Enoch's view as if she had been a nosegay) ! '
All unwittingly, he has that charm which
no knowledge of the world can buy, of guile-
lessness, trust, and of falling in love to an
entirely ridiculous extent. As for the
harum-scarum, fickle Bob, never to be de-
pended on save for susceptibility, an indifference to being slashed about in his country's
cause, and a capacity for being deceived in
every port, I fear most readers repeat the
unjust judgment of fate, and elect him over
the head of the steadfast trumpet-major.

Of the young men of more serious, weight-
ier cast, besides Giles and Gabriel, first, for
vitality and interest, come John Loveday,
Clym, and Angel Clare, the gentleman, the
idealist, and the theorist. Clym Yeobright
is, of all types of character, the least reward-
ing to his inventor, unless he be given a big
world to live in. A man of intellect and
ideals working in a narrow sphere is apt to
appear as a coxcomb and not to be believed
in. Clym is believed in, partly because his
intellectual capacities are so divorced from
ambition, and so singularly wedded to
Nature, that life in the narrow world of
Egdon seems quite congruous, but also because of a certain intensity of feeling which
has been used in his making, as if a bit of
his creator had been infused into him, and
breathed through him. Angel is of more
contradictory tendencies, and less precise
effect. While interested lookers on at Tess's
tragedy have rushed to vehement and oppo-
site conclusions about him, Mr. Hardy has

left his own judgment in a half light; has
pointed out his limitations, but with a kind
of understanding pity for him, and refused
to make him the scape-goat to bear the sins
of the prejudices of the world. Angel is a
skilful embodiment of a type of the modern
man in any age, one whose mind has perceived more truth than his soul will ever
grasp, whose intelligence has outstripped
the capacities of his nature.

Among the older men two gloomy figures
stand out, Boldwood and Henchard. Boldwood, the still, deep man, on whom life
makes so few and such ineffaceable impressions, is built in a simpler fashion than most
of Mr. Hardy's characters. He is no more
real than Heathcliff, for all that he is made
after a more human pattern ; but his reality
is not less. Henchard, that strange bar-
barian, love, generosity, and the nobler
virtues as much stronger in him as jealousy,
recklessness, thunderous temper, and caprice
are weaker in the smoother, better-drilled

folks around him, is the type of the makers of catastrophes,—broken in for a time to the routine of civilisation, even in the newer paths he ruled, but his natural self was bound to break the bands eventually. His figure stands by itself strongly defined and lonely, not only in Maumsbury Ring and on Egdon, but among all Mr. Hardy's other characters, and among those of English fiction.

Among the older men, too, should be remembered Parson Clare, he who 'loved Paul ' of Tarsus, liked St. John, hated St. James ' as much as he dared.' Narrow in opinion, incapable of subtlety, hard in theory, yet with a heart broadened by charity for the sinner, his was a nature that no mental austerity could make other than sweet. He is not treated very dramatically; but the description of him is so vivid and beautiful that one is fain to give him a place in one's memory with the 'poure Persoun of a toun,' and with him of Auburn.

A few classifications, references, and selected portraits, do not cover the ground of Mr. Hardy's success as a character-painter. And in the description of the personages that are not dramatic successes there is always much first-hand observation. On looking back at his folk, merry and sad, gentle and rebel, simple and sophisticated, one's first thought is that they are stimulating company ; the second, that, read by other eyes, many of them might have seemed commonplace enough. Out of the variety which is their chief characteristic is evolved the truth, that emotions and complexities, varied mental and moral features, are not dependent on a highly organised civilisation for their existence, that if the society-mill has a refining, it has also an effacing power.

H

HUMOURIST

VI

HUMOURIST

THERE are two widely different grounds on which Mr. Hardy may be considered as a humourist. He has one obvious, even assertive claim to the title, founded on what if it be not humour is naught, and it is convenient to give this claim first attention. The Weatherbury, Mellstock, Egdon, and Overcombe rustics, are mainly the channels through which his more evident humour flows. His attitude towards country life counts for a good deal in its quality; he takes his stand just enough outside to watch with a keen relish the differences between rustic ways and the smoother life of towns, and just enough inside to miss none of the fine shades, and to mix no contempt with his sense of the ludicrous. This humour is mainly concerned with the surface of life, though it takes occasional dips below. The eccentricities of rustic manners and rustic facial expressions are noted with the relentless momentary truth of a Dutch painter. All the topsy-turvydom of simple minds brought face to face with novel experiences or unfamiliar ideas, asserting their real dignity somewhat unreally by misfitting words and wandering metaphors, are grist to the mill of this lighter humour, which is at its richest in ' Under the Greenwood Tree ' and ' Far from the Madding Crowd.' He has given us less of it of late years, though in ' A Few Crusted Characters ' there is a revival.

It reaches us by a kind of translation. To live a year in Wessex would mean certain failure in finding Henery, or Spinks, or Poorgrass. To live ten, with ear and understanding capable of being acclimatised, would probably be to find them living with a numerous kindred. Mr. Hardy has his own way of presenting the local accent of mind and speech and habit, so that when it reaches us it may be essentially, if not literally, true. It is not the only method, but it is a vivid one. Shakespeare uses the same; to a smaller extent Scott does so also, but he trusts more to literalness. In mentioning Shakespeare I do not allude to certain epigrammatic phrasings, turns of speech, or of events, that have the look of distinct imitation, like the scene in the vault, where the familiar discussion takes place between Worm and Cannister and the elder Smith, on the noble dead in the coffins, or the tranter's description of the varying symptoms of love, or his exposition of ' " how a ' maiden is. She'll swear she's dying for ' thee, and she is dying for thee, and ' she will die for thee ; but she 'll fling a look ' over t' other shoulder at another young ' feller, though never leaving off dying for

' thee just the same," ' or Liddy's reflection
on how sweet it would be to be able to dis-
dain a suitor's offer with ' "No, sir—I 'm your
' better," ' or ' " kiss my foot, sir ; my face is
' for mouths of consequence," ' all made after
an older generation stage pattern. Apart
from what may possibly be an effect of memory, there is an essential likeness. Poorgrass and the Maltster, and Cantle and Leaf,
and Matthew Moon, are of the kindred of
Bottom, and Launce, and Launcelot Gobbo,
and of the clown who was the lover of Mopsa
and the dupe of Autolycus. They are clowns,
compounds of wit and simplicity, with no
clear dividing line between the qualities.

This may be but another way of saying
that they are caricatures, but if so, I am not
consciously depreciating them. Caricature
may, unjustly, bear the reproach of its
grosser manifestations, but it is as legitimate
a process of art as symbolism, or any other
adaptation of literal or spiritual facts for the
more striking presentation of some portion

of them. It consists merely in the isolation
of certain qualities or contrasts from the
softening, behazing atmosphere through
which literal eyes behold them, and which
is everyday-life's means of spoiling a joke.
Not that everyday life always insists on making use of the hazy medium. As caricature
and farce must be classed a good part of the
humour of the Weatherbury rustics and their
fellows. The tales of Tony Kytes and
Andrey Satchell, the mission of the Mellstock choir to the Vicar, Cainy Ball's visit to
Bath, are all farce, the last very broad farce.
But the fun is genuine, the absurdity is
essentially true to human nature, and the
laugh it raises very genial. To live in the
tranter's company is to love country ways
ever after. The narrative of Bob Loveday's
return, too, is enough to convert a cynic. It
is one of the best examples of that mingled
geniality and piquancy, where laughing at
and with the actors are so skilfully combined,
one adding to the effect of the other. But it

is not brief enough for quoting in full, and it
will not bear division.

The geniality of country ways he shows
occasionally interspersed with disciplinary
candour.   Mr. Maybold was sensitive under
its   touch,   but   did   not   resent   it—'The
' ancient body of minstrels in the passage
' felt their curiosity surging higher and
' higher as the minutes passed. . . . Yet their
' sense of propriety would probably have re-
' strained them from any attempt to discover
' what was going on in the study, had not the
' Vicar's pen fallen to the floor.   The con-
' viction that the movement of chairs, etc.,
' necessitated by the search, could only have
' been caused by the catastrophe of a bloody
' fight, overpowered all other considerations ;
' and they advanced to the door, which had
' only just fallen to.   Thus, when Mr. May-
' bold raised his eyes after the stooping, he
' beheld glaring through the door Mr. Penny
' in full-length portraiture, Mail's face and
' shoulders above Mr. Penny's head, Spinks's
' forehead and eyes over Mail's crown, and a

' fractional part of Bowman's countenance
' under Spinks's arm—crescent shaped por-
' tions of other heads and faces being visible
' behind these—the whole dozen and odd
' eyes bristling with eager inquiry.

' Mr. Penny, as is the case with excitable
' bootmakers and men, on seeing the Vicar
' look at him, and hearing no word spoken,
' thought it incumbent upon himself to say
' something of any kind. Nothing suggested
' itself till he had looked for about half a
' minute at the Vicar.

' "You'll excuse my naming it, sir," he
' said, regarding with much commiseration
' the mere surface of the Vicar's face, " but
' perhaps you don't know, sir, that your chin
' have bust out a-bleeding where you cut
' yourself a-shaving this morning, sir." . . .

' " Dear me, dear me ! " said Mr. Maybold
' hastily, looking very red, and brushing his
' chin with his hand, then taking out his
' handkerchief and wiping the place.

' "That's it, sir ; all right again now, 'a

' b'lieve—a mere nothing," said Mr. Penny.
' " A little bit of fur off your hat will stop it in
' a minute, if it should bust out again."

' " I 'll let ye have a bit of fur off mine,"
' said Reuben, to show his good feeling.'

Oak has to bear this candour too, and he
does so with his usual good sense.   On occa-
sion his own tongue was plain enough.

' " Ay, I can mind yer face now, shepherd,"
' said Henery Fray, criticising Gabriel with
' misty eyes as he entered upon his second
' tune. " Yes—now I see ye blowing into the
' flute I know ye to be the same man I see
' play at Casterbridge, for yer mouth were
' scrimped up and yer eyes a-staring out like
' a strangled man's—just as they be now."

' " 'Tis a pity that playing the flute should
' make a man look such a scarecrow," ob-
' served Mr. Mark Clark, with additional criti-
' cism of Gabriel's countenance, the latter
' person jerking out, with the ghastly grimace
' required by the instrument, the chorus of
' ' Dame Durden.' . . ."

' " I hope you don't mind that young man
' Mark Clark's bad manners in naming your
' features?" whispered Joseph to Gabriel
' privately.

' " Not at all," said Mr. Oak.

' " For by nature ye be a very handsome
' man, shepherd," continued Joseph Poor-
' grass, with winning suavity.

' " Ay, that ye be," said the company.

' " Thank you very much," said Oak, in
' the modest tone good manners demanded,
' thinking, however, that he would never let
' Bathsheba see him playing the flute.'

Oak, however, in his robustness, was a
fitter subject for plain speaking than Christian Cantle, who was, nevertheless, fated to
endure much of it—

' " Yes; ' No moon, no man.' 'Tis one of
' the truest sayings ever spit out. The boy
' never comes to anything that 's born at new
' moon. A bad job for thee, Christian, that
' you should have showed your nose then of
' all days in the month."

' " 1 suppose the moon was terrible full
' when you were born ? " said Christian, with
' a look of hopeless admiration at Fairway.

' " Well, 'a was not new," Mr. Fairway re-
plied, with a disinterested gaze.

' " I 'd sooner go without drink at Lammas-
' tide than be a man of no moon," continued
' Christian, in the same shattered recitative.
' " 'Tis said I be only the rames of a man,
' and no good in the world at all ! "

Humour of this conscious kind, much of
it expressing itself purposely by an artificial
method, has its dangers, and Mr. Hardy has
not always escaped them.   There is an
occasional difficulty in the joking.   And any
lack of genuine fun in an intentionally humorous scene is more evident in a novel of
everyday life than would be the case in the
more artificial setting of a stage drama.
Some drolleries, too, that raise a smile
quickly enough, suggest immediate acknow-
ledgment to the author at the back of the
speaker rather than to the speaker himself.

It is on this lighter side of Mr. Hardy's comedy that his only evident resemblance —and it is but a faint one—to George Eliot comes in. The shrewd or cynical things he putsintorusticmouths, like '"Yes, matrimony 'do begin 'Dearly Beloved,' and ends wi' ' 'Amazement,' as the prayer book says" ; ' or ' "Doom ? Doom is nothing beside a elderly 'woman ";' or ' " Enteren the Church is the 'ruin of a man's wit, for wit's nothen with-'out a faint shadder o' sin,"' have a hint of the mind that created Mrs. Poyser. But Mr. Hardy's rustics speak their epigrams out of rather more reckless hearts.

Perhaps to find a purpose for his wit and high spirits should be a disqualification for writing a chapter on a humourist at all. Yet, consciously or not, they are part of the plan of the novels. The most susceptible reader will probably drop few tears over Mr. Hardy's stories. Pathos is not wanting, especially in his later books, but it is kept under, and utters itself unwillingly, as often as not in mockery or irony. One sin he has not committed; he has never been maudlin. And much of the sadness he expresses is of a kind tears do not come to relieve. Of that gentle pathos which is often the to-morrow of tragedy, or its pitying neighbour, you find little. But relief there must be, else the tension would be intolerable, and it comes in fun and farce, where these are congruous, or in irony of tone and circumstance.

Before considering his other claim to be regarded as a humourist, it is well to face the assertion that he is not one, for it has been made. Not that any argument is of use in a matter to which no recognisable laws can be applied. If the humour of the Wessex clowns be artificial and an acquired taste, it is well for the spirits and the lungs of the general that it is not too difficult of acquisition; and there we must leave it. But the assertion includes not only an inaptitude to be amused by the Weatherbury wits but a contemptuous amusement in the wrong place. A favourite example of his lack of humour is the talk of the dairy-maids concerning Angel Clare. Their conversation shows a want of the quality on their part, poor things. But that was a symptom of their malady : how many are the happily-constituted mortals who can combine the being desperately in love with a sense of the ludicrous? Perhaps Mr. Hardy here furnished matter for a smile, not a very broad one, without hoisting a signal of his intention—very bad policy, of course. But I venture the suggestion diffidently, for that there are lapses in the humour cannot be denied. Knight and Fitzpiers suffer from such, and so does the whole of 'A Laodicean.' The lapses are infrequent, however, and always strike a sympathetic reader as un-characteristic.

It is possible to have a very hearty appreciation of the Wessex clowns and wits, and of their excellent fooling, and yet think

I

Mr. Hardy has better claims to the title of
humourist than as being their creator. The
general attitude of the novels towards life is
that of a humourist. Indeed one might
almost look on his tragedies as his translations of the immortals' sense of humour and
their manner of ghastly jesting. But, at
least, with few exceptions, he has his eye
always on the comedy of circumstances.
Some of the novels, like ' Two on a Tower,'
lack humour in the detail, but have it in the
central conception. There is abundance of
it of an ironical kind in the contrast between
Swithin and his lady, her passions burning
hot at an earthly level, his flashing a cold
keen light away among the Immensities.
The whole of ' The Hand of Ethelberta ' is
a light satire on the absurd conventions that
have given to class distinctions a sanctity
no religion has ever won. ' Under the
Greenwood Tree ' and ' The Trumpet
Major ' are comedies throughout, written
n a laughing mood, though there are sug-

gestions of gravity in the latter. If there were no Weatherbury rustics to make mirth, ' Far from the Madding Crowd ' would still be a fine comedy. Bathsheba is better than the sum of all their wit or absurdity. She is looked at and watched and dissected by a humourist, a humane humourist. The incident of her quarrel with Gabriel after he had reproved her for encouraging Boldwood, her dismissal of him, the loss of her sheep, her appeal to him to return, and her reconciliation—a finely compounded mixture of interested and tender motives— could only have been drawn by a humourist of rare and delicate touch.

This attitude is less evident in ' Desperate Remedies,' in ' The Woodlanders,' in ' The Return of the Native,' and 'Tess,' if the sport of circumstances with poor human nature be not admitted as a manifestation of the quality. In ' A Group of Noble Dames ' the humour is wrought in with the telling of the stories ; in ' Life's

Little Ironies' it is not lacking, but it is gall to the taste ; there is something tonic in the gall, nevertheless.

Into much of the most vigorous humour there enters a certain grimness. Perhaps the finest bit of comedy in the novels is the scene in 'The Three Strangers' where the escaped convict waves cups with the hangman, and sings in his deep bass the chorus to the hangman's ghastly song, 'And on his 'soul may God ha' mercy.' The journey of Sol Chickerel with his prospective and undesired noble brother-in-law would make a good second, but there are rivals for the place. There is nothing comic about Wildeve and the reddleman's game of dice by the light of the glowworms on the heath, yet it is comedy all the same, of a sardonic kind.

But Mr. Hardy's greatest manifestation of humour, outside purely amusing scenes, is in his conception of Henchard. Like all barbarians, the man shows as a great jest against the tameness, the low-spirited reason-

ableness of ordinary life. Wherever you
look at him this jest is inextricably mixed
with the tragic about him ; and I think no
defence is needed for quoting, as illustrative
of his author's humour, the scene of the ex-
mayor's Sunday visit to the King of Prussia,
where he demands music from the assembled
choir-members—'hymns, ballets, or ranti-
' pole rubbish ; the Rogue's March or the
cherubim's warble '—and then turns his
craving for harmony into a savage demand
that they should curse his rival :—

' " As 'tis Sunday, neighbours, suppose we
' raise the Fourth Psa'am to Samuel Wakely's
' tune, as improved by me ? " ' said the leader.

' " Hang Samuel Wakely's tune, as im-
' proved by thee ! " said Henchard. " Chuck
' across one of your psalters—old Wiltshire is
' the only tune worth singing—the psalm-tune
' that would make my blood ebb and flow
' like the sea when I was a steady chap.
' I 'll find some words to fit en." ' The
words he finds are the terrible ones, ' His

seed shall orphans be,' ending with the
ghastly triumph—

> ' And the next age his hated name
> Shall utterly deface.'

"" I know the Psa'am—I know the Psa'am !"
' said the leader hastily ; "but I would as lief
' not sing it. 'Twasn't made for singing.
' We chose it once when the gipsies stole
' the pa'son's mare, thinking to please him,
' but he were quite upset.   Whatever Servant
' David were thinking about when he made
' a Psalm that nobody can sing without dis-
' gracing himself, I can't fathom !   Now
' then, the Fourth Psalm to Samuel Wakely's
' tune, as improved by me."

' "'Od seize your sauce—I tell ye to sing
' the Hundred and Ninth, to Wiltshire, and
' sing it you shall ! " roared Henchard. " Not
' a single one of all the droning crew of ye
' goes out of this room till that Psalm is
' sung !"   He slipped off the table, seized
' the poker, and, going to the door, placed his
' back against it.   " Now then, go ahead, if

' you don't wish to have your cust pates
' broken !"

' " Don't 'ee, don't 'ee take on so !—As 'tis
' the Sabbath day, and 'tis Servant David's
' words and not ours, perhaps we don't mind
' for once, hey ? " said one of the terrified
' choir, looking round upon the rest. So the
' instruments were tuned and the com-
' minatory verses sung.

' " Thank ye, thank ye," said Henchard in
' a softened voice, his eyes growing downcast,
' and his manner that of a man much moved
' by the strains. " Don't you blame David,"
' he went on in low tones, shaking his head
' without raising his eyes. " He knew what
' he was about when he wrote that. If I
' could afford it, be hanged if I wouldn't
' keep a church choir at my own expense to
' play and sing to me at these low, dark times
' of my life. But the bitter thing is, that when
' I was rich I didn't need what I could have,
' and now I be poor I can't have what I
' need !" '

The essential quality in this passage springs from the same deep underground root as poetry and tragedy, and Mr. Hardy has revealed enough of it from time to time to give him honourable rank among the greater humourists.

PROSE WRITER

VII

PROSE WRITER

IN popular meaning, style is a convenient
quality, enabling one to make a guessing
recognition of a writer without looking at
his title-page, readily supplying adjectives
for conversation, like 'obscure,' 'subtle,' or
'affected,' and suggesting mental efforts on
the surface quite apart from the thinking-
task the surface may enclose. 'Stylist' is
too ugly a word to be grudged to those
whose writing exactly fulfils these conditions :
the masters of style in England, save only
three or four whose eccentricities have been
the inevitable expression of their genius,

have no mannerisms, perhaps not much superficial individuality; they cannot be neatly summed up in a descriptive phrase as guarantee they have been read, but they have a language at command commensurate with the force, and harmonious with the tone of the ideas they seek to express. Mr. Hardy is no 'stylist,' perhaps less so than most writers of to-day. The consistency of the inner ideas, their variety, too, and the vividness of his imagination are his recognisable qualities.

But just as far as from extreme individualism is his style removed from that impersonal manner, the manner of Miss Austen and all the story-tellers pure and simple, where poetical and rhythmical phrasing are eschewed, and an occasional dry epigram or a palpable antithesis the only ornaments allowed. Fiction to-day, uttering much that was formerly expressed by poetry, the drama, and the other forms of the criticism of life, has borrowed from them their richness and variety of pattern. Mr. Hardy's style reflects too much of his own personality to be of the neutral, colourless order. But it is not a livery; it is rather a series of garments waiting on his moods, and an examination of them would be describable by the most contradictory phrases. He is far from being an even writer. You may confidently seek in his stories some of the most beautiful and vigorous English prose of the century, and in the track of it you will run up and down almost every conceivable altitude. A master of style he is not, for, save in his shorter stories, he does not master it. It does not run away with him, as with overfluent writers, but it stiffens into rigidity sometimes, and he cannot shake it into freedom.

It reaches its height in certain tragic passages of his greater novels, and in descriptions of natural beauty in all of them; but it is most consistently admirable in his shorter tales. There he is unsurpassed for the very qualities unhappily absent from much of his other work, for lightness, deftness, grace. Setting aside two or three that are a trifle flat in treatment, like 'Fellow-Townsmen,' 'Interlopers at the Knap,' and 'The Winters and the Palmeys,' it would be difficult to find in English or any other fiction more admirable craftsmanship. Their precise and delicate art reaches its consummation where tragedy or any very deep human interest, if present, is, at least, not uppermost, when he is in a bantering mood, playing with the humours and the ironies of life. There are no more deftly-told stories in the language than 'The First Countess of Wessex' and 'Lady Mottisfont,' more vigorous than 'The Three Strangers,' more fascinating than 'The Distracted Preacher.' And not these only, but others, too, are admirable in their proportions, in their simplicity, and their restraint. In his lighter, brighter moods he is like a sophisticated Goldsmith.

Yet there is a good deal in Mr. Hardy's writing for which only all the interest of the story and characters can compensate. The rigidity that marked 'Desperate Remedies' crops up again and again; especially is it felt in 'A Laodicean,' the least pliant of all, though it must be owned there is a certain consistency between the *parvenue* Paula, always standing on her uncertain dignity, and such a sentence as this: ' The ostensible ease with which she drew ' them into a bye conversation had perhaps ' the defect of proving too much : though ' her tacit contention that no love was in ' question was not incredible on the sup- ' position that affronted pride alone caused ' her embarrassment'; and knowing the invariable correctness of Somerset's demeanour, we resign ourselves to hearing his strength of mind, after Paula had been very rude to him, expressed as a resolution 'to ' persevere in the heretofore satisfactory ' paths of art while life and faculties were

' left, though every instant must proclaim
' that there would be no longer any col-
' lateral attraction in that pursuit.'   Other
writers have fits of carelessness, when they
are slipshod and vapid.   When Mr. Hardy
nods, he seems to sit particularly bolt
upright, to pick his words and construct
his sentences with more than ordinary
elaboration.   When he is bored he becomes
formal, not listless.   This kind of thing
reappears almost every time conventional
experiences, or incidents, or characters are
dealt with; whenever, in short, he has
imperfect sympathy with his subject.   But
imperfect sympathy does not explain it all.
Very charmingly is Grace Melbury presented; but the description is prefaced by
a sentence or two that put readers out of
tune for the good ones that follow.   'From
' the highest point of view, to precisely
' describe a human being, the focus of a
' universe, how impossible !   But, apart from
' transcendentalism, there never probably

'lived a person who was in herself more
'completely a *reductio ad absurdum* of at-
'tempts to appraise a woman, even ex-
'ternally, by items of face and figure.'

The technicalities, the tags of philosophi-
cal, theological, and scientific reading that
obtrude themselves from time to time are
less objectionable. They are never quite
irrelevant. Angel's vocabulary, indeed,
sounds unnecessarily high and extensive
heard in the neighbourhood of a dairy;
but, as in Paula's case, there is a fitness in
it, for, after all, he was brother of the man
who took 'A Counterblast to Agnosticism'
on a walking-tour. Perhaps it is only
where the pedantic language is used in
dealing with unlearned human nature that
one seriously wishes it away. Simple
organisms under the microscope of the
scientist form the abundant material on
which his learning and intellect are exercised. In imaginative literature something
of the same kind must occasionally take

K

place; but the microscope and the method
and vocabulary of science need not be too
visible and audible.   The vivid result in
broad plain language is all that need appear.
A flash or two of poetic insight does the
thing most fittingly.

But having said that he has unhappy
moments when his pen is formal and
pedantic, and that only in a few of his
books is there any evenness of delight,
the rest of one's space is needed to point to
his excellencies.   It is a robust language he
writes, never hazy, never wanting in grip.
His lines are sure, and his acid bites deep.
Take the picture of Henchard and his wife
on their way to Weydon Priors fair.   How
admirably precise are all the essentials, how
firm is the step of the narrative, a swinging
gait, with lightness in it, and swayed con-
stantly by the thoughts within !   Any page
whatsoever of 'The Trumpet Major' would
serve as a model of trained and vigorous
story-writing, so brisk and snell is it, so

clear-sounding and assured. Anne watching the *Victory* sail away with Nelson and
Hardy and Bob on board will serve as
example of his tensity and definiteness of
expression: 'The wild, herbless, weather-
' worn promontory was quite a solitude, and,
' saving the one old lighthouse about fifty
' yards up the slope, scarce a mark was
' visible to show that humanity had ever
' been near the spot. Anne found herself a
' seat on a stone, and swept with her eyes the
' tremulous expanse of water around her that
' seemed to utter a ceaseless unintelligible
' incantation. . . The great silent ship, with
' her population of blue jackets, marines,
' officers, captain, and the admiral who was
' not to return alive, passed like a phantom
' the meridian of the Bill. Sometimes her
' aspect was that of a large white bat, some-
' times that of a grey one. In the course of
' time the watching girl saw that the ship had
' passed her nearest point; the breadth of
' her sails diminished by foreshortening, till

'she assumed the form of an egg on end.
'After this something seemed to twinkle;
'and Anne, who had previously withdrawn
'from the old sailor, went back to him, and
'looked again through the glass. The
'twinkling was the light falling upon the
'cabin windows of the ship's stern. She ex-
'plained it to the old man.

'"Then we see now what the enemy have
'seen but once. That was in seventy-nine,
'when she sighted the French and Spanish
'fleet off Scilly, and she retreated because
'she feared a landing. Well, 'tis a brave
'ship, and she carries brave men!"'...

'The *Victory* was fast dropping away.
'She was on the horizon, and soon appeared
'hull down. That seemed to be like the
'beginning of a greater end than her present
'vanishing. Anne Garland could not stay
'by the sailor any longer, and went about
'a stone's-throw off, where she was hidden
'by the inequality of the cliff from his view.
'The vessel was now exactly end on, and

' stood out in the direction of the Start, her
' width having contracted to the proportion
' of a feather. . . .

'The courses of the *Victory* were absorbed
' into the main, then her top-sails went, and
' then her top-gallants. She was now no
' more than a dead fly's wing on a sheet of
' spider's web; and even this fragment
' diminished. Anne could hardly bear to
' see the end, and yet she resolved not to
' flinch. The admiral's flag sank behind
' the watery line, and in a minute the very
' truck of the last topmast stole away. The
' *Victory* was gone.

'Anne's lip quivered as she murmured,
' without removing her wet eyes from the
' vacant and solemn horizon, " ' They that
' go down to the sea in ships, that do busi-
' ness in great waters—— ' "

' " ' These see the works of the Lord, and
' His wonders in the deep,' " was returned
' by a man's voice from behind her.'

Examples of his style at its best are

examples of other gifts, too, which it is still more interesting to exemplify. This chapter, therefore, may rest with its general statements hardly at all served by particular instances. Elsewhere, serving another purpose, these will be found, and will prove that, notwithstanding his occasional awkward carefulness and formality of language, his wideawake manner of dosing, Mr. Hardy has the strongest claims to be counted among the writers of fine prose in this century. He uses no catchwords; he has no tricks; no affectations; there is nothing cheap in what he has written. He has the ambition of a writer of romance and a poet to reveal passion and beauty and despair, the heart of man and the face of the world, and his best revelations have a sure preservative in the force, variety, and sincerity of his expression.

PAINTER OF NATURE

VIII

PAINTER OF NATURE

As an interpreter of the world out of doors, Mr. Hardy has no equal among English prose writers. At single points in the capacity for revealing Nature, many touch him. His greatest contemporary in English fiction has as much sympathy and perhaps as deep insight, but has not recorded his vision with such clearness. Jefferies and Kingsley were naturalists with poets' eyes, but neither approaches him in producing broad effects, or in the interpretation of the character of landscape. His reflective spirit abroad in the outer world puts one sometimes in mind of Thoreau, but in

Thoreau the brightness and colour are mainly
in his own reflections : he reveals little in
the outside things he chronicles. Hardy is
more profitably compared with some poets,
and allowing for differences of phrase and
tone, the writer of late days whom he most
resembles in his method of transcribing
Nature is Tennyson. The intimate glance, as
peering as a naturalist's, and as quick to see
details, yet concerned mainly to extract the
beauty and the character of the objects or
the landscape, is the same. The balance
for perfection of expression is on the side of
the poet, for prose is but an awkward medium
after all ; but Tennyson best used this gift
in registering single events in Nature rather
than pervading moods, and the temperament of the outside world, combined with
the signs by which it is expressed, he has
never put into words as Mr. Hardy has
done.

With Tennyson, Nature is a thing to be
rejoiced in, to be learnt by constant glances,

like the face of the beloved. With the novelist it is so, too, but still more is it a thing to live in sympathy with, or at least on terms of closest intimacy, a thing not only with a face but a heart as well. Nevertheless, it is to the school of Tennyson, rather than the less realistic one of Wordsworth, that Mr. Hardy is attached. His descriptive passages are an integral portion of the stories. You may know your Balzac, having skipped, out of the whole, what would amount to volumes, but you cannot know the Wessex novels with proportionate omissions. His landscapes are not even appropriate backgrounds merely, but living personalities that take sides or play the chorus to the drama. They are never vague. They arrest your attention as a keen-sighted friend who should point with his staff to what was happening along the road, or hush your chatter and make you listen. They are not merely illustrative of observation, but are essentially pictorial. You feel it is by the merest chance they are not in colour rather than in printer's ink. Perhaps it is this painter's way of looking at things, this instinct of concentrating enthusiasm into the interpretation of such form and tone as shall express both fact and sentiment, that has prevented him from bursting into poetical measures to sing the joy of the beauty.

The knowledge with which he endows Angel, of 'the seasons in their moods, morn- ' ing and evening, night and noon, in their ' temperaments; winds in their several dispo- ' sitions; trees, waters, and clouds, shades ' and silences, *ignes fatui* ; constellations, and ' the voices of inanimate things,' is his own. ' The Woodlanders ' is a calendar of wood- land life. He tells the clock by out-of-doors methods. There is a time of day written on his every landscape, and every time of day he has chronicled, from ' the twilight of the ' morning, in the violet or pink dawn,' till day has passed and night has come again. Here is one out of many morning pictures : ' The

' gray half-tones of daybreak are not the
' gray half-tones of the day's close, though
' the degree of their shade may be the same.
' In the twilight of the morning light seems
' active, darkness passive ; in the twilight of
' evening it is the darkness which is active
' and crescent, and the light which is the
' drowsy reverse. . . .

  ' The mixed, singular, luminous gloom in
' which they walked along together to the
' spot where the cows lay, often made him
' think of the Resurrection hour . . . Whilst
' all the landscape was in neutral shade his
' companion's face, which was the focus of
' his eyes, rising above the mist stratum,
' seemed to have a sort of phosphorescence
' upon it. She looked ghostly, as if she were
' merely a soul at large.' There follows on
this passage a marvellous picture of the life
abroad at this non-human hour.

  Night, that strange personality, has had its
heart read again and again in ' The Woodlanders ' and ' The Return of the Native,'

but never has it been laid more open than in
the picture of Oak at midnight on Nor-
combe Ewelease. A sentence or two may
serve as a reminder to turn and read the
the whole again. 'Beneath this half-wooded,
' half-naked hill, and the vague, still horizon
' that its summit indistinctly commanded,
' was a mysterious sheet of fathomless shade—
' the sounds from which suggested that what
' it concealed bore some resemblance to
' features here. The thin grasses, more or
' less coating the hill, were touched by the
' wind in breezes of differing powers, and
' almost of differing natures—one rubbing
' the blades heavily, another raking them
' piercingly, another brushing them like a
' soft broom. The instinctive act of human-
' kind was to stand and listen, and learn how
' the trees on the right and the trees on the
' left wailed or chaunted to each other in
' the regular antiphonies of a cathedral choir;
' how hedges and other shapes to leeward
' then caught the note, lowering it to the

' tenderest sob ; and how the hurrying gust
' then plunged to the south, to be heard no
' more. . . . To persons standing on a hill
' during a clear midnight such as this, the
' roll of the world eastward is almost a pal-
' pable movement. . . . Whatever be its
' origin, the impression of riding along is
' vivid and abiding.'

Though he has followed Nature's gayer
moods with blitheness, as his strongest human
note is tragedy, so is his greatest Nature
revelation that of the earth in her sterner
phases. He has made ' haggard Egdon '
for ever unforgetable.

' The spot was, indeed, a near relation of
' night, and, when night showed itself, an
' apparent tendency to gravitate together
' could be perceived in its shades and the
' scene. The sombre stretch of rounds and
' hollows seemed to rise and meet the even-
' ing gloom in pure sympathy, the heath ex-
' haling darkness as rapidly as the heavens
' precipitated it. . . . The place became

' full of a watchful intentness now ; for when
' other things sank brooding to sleep, the
' heath appeared slowly to awake and listen.
' Every night its Titanic form seemed to
' await something ; but it had waited thus,
' unmoved, during so many centuries, through
' the crises of so many things, that it could
' only be imagined to await one last crisis—
' the final overthrow. . . . During winter
' darkness, tempests, and mists. . . . Egdon
' was roused to reciprocity ; for it may be
' said that the storm was its lover, and the
' wind its friend.   Then it became the home
' of strange phantoms ; and it was found to
' be the hitherto unrecognised original of
' those wild regions of obscurity which are
' vaguely felt to be compassing us about in
' midnight dreams of flight and disaster,
' and are never thought of after the dream
' till revived by scenes like this.   .   .   .
' As with some persons who have long
' lived their lives apart, solitude seemed to
' look out of its countenance.   It had a

' lonely face, suggesting tragical possibili-
' ties.'

There is hardly a natural event that in
more than one aspect he has not chronicled.
The rain-storm in ' Under the Greenwood
Tree' is as true to fact as anything he has
done later, but the memorable storm-picture
is that of Oak and Bathsheba saving the
ricks. From Troy's senseless revelry Oak
goes out into the night, and finds one, then
another and another message from the Great
Mother of strange things coming to pass : the
toad crossing the path, the slug seeking in-
door refuge, the terror of the sheep—

'Time went on, and the moon vanished
' not to reappear. It was the farewell of the
' ambassador previous to war. The night had
' a haggard look, like a sick thing ; and there
' came finally an utter expiration of air from
' the whole heaven in the form of a slow
' breeze, which might have been likened
' to a death. . . . Heaven opened then,
' indeed. . . . It was a perfect dance of

L

'death. The forms of skeletons appeared
'in the air, shaped with blue fire for bones—
'dancing, leaping, striding, racing around,
'and mingling altogether in unparalleled
'confusion. With these were intertwined un-
'dulating snakes of green. Behind these was
'a broad mass of lesser light. . . . Oak had
'hardly time to gather up these impressions
'into a thought, and to see how strangely
'the red feather of her hat shone in this
'light, when the tall tree on the hill before-
'mentioned seemed on fire to a white heat,
'and a new one among these terrible voices
'mingled with the last crash of those preced-
'ing. It was a stupefying blast, harsh and
'pitiless, and it fell upon their ears in a dead,
'flat blow, without that reverberation which
'lends the tones of a drum to more distant
'thunder.'

Sensitive discrimination of the ear is a
rarer endowment than that of the eye. You
feel it is his in the opening lines of 'Under
'the Greenwood Tree,' in the song at night

among the water-meadows in 'The Mayor of
Casterbridge,' but its triumph is in his translation of the wind over Egdon—

'Gusts in innumerable series followed each
'other from the north-west, and when each
'one of them raced past, the sound of its
'progress resolved into three. Treble, tenor,
'and bass notes were to be found therein.
'The general ricochet of the whole over pits
'and prominences had the gravest pitch of
'the chime. Next there could be heard
'the baritone buzz of a holly-tree. Below
'these in force, above them in pitch, a
'dwindled voice strove hard at a husky tune,
'which was the peculiar local sound alluded
'to '—that is, the sound of the wind in the
heather—like 'the ruins of human song
'which remain to the throat of fourscore and
'ten. It was a worn whisper, dry and papery,
'and it brushed so distinctly across the ear
'that, by the accustomed, the material minu-
'tiæ in which it originated could be realised
'as by touch. . . . One inwardly saw the

' infinity of those combined multitudes ; and
' perceived that each of the tiny trumpets
' was seized on, entered, scoured and
' emerged from by the wind as thoroughly as
' if it were as vast as a crater.

' " The spirit moved them." '

He is a great pleinairist, occasionally
content to render only colour and facts, but
far more often painting landscape broadly,
with a perfect eye not only for topographical
features, but for the character to be read in
the lines, and for the mood in the tones of
the atmosphere. The picture of Sherton in
early autumn, of Ethelberta's view from the
giant's grave over Purbeck, the description of the kindly languorous Vale of Blackmore, and of the sparkling valley of the
Great Dairies, can hardly pass out of the
mind of those to whom natural beauty
appeals ; and how rarely can that be said of
pictures made in words !

His treatment of landscape is more than
pictorial : it is sometimes dramatic. A very

casual reading of the stories will leave in the memory, apart from general impressions, a larger number of clearly defined scenes in which time and place and circumstance agree to make a climax of picturesqueness, than will the works of almost any other writer of fiction. Anne Garland looking from the mill towards the down where the scattering of the sheep tells of the first arrival of the soldiers ; the dark figure seen by the reddle-man on the barrow against the night sky ; the dairyman and maids creeping along the meads to discover the noxious weed that gave the butter a 'twang,' flash up on the memory at once. So does the picture of Stonehenge, before the policemen come on the scene—their advent is unforgiveable : why didn't Tess and Angel double, and get caught in Old Sarum ? But the most mas-terly of all such pictures is that of the turnip-field at Flintcomb Ash—

'The swede-field in which she and her ' companion were set hacking was a stretch

' of a hundred odd acres, in one patch, on
' the highest ground of the farm, rising
' above stony lanchets or lynchets—the out-
' crop of siliceous veins in the chalk forma-
' tion, composed of myriads of loose white
' flints in bulbous, cusped, and phallic
' shapes. The upper half of each turnip
' had been eaten off by the live-stock, and
' it was the business of the two women to
' grub up the lower or earthy half of the
' root with a hooked fork called a hacker,
' that it might be eaten also. Every leaf of
' the vegetable having already been con-
' sumed, the whole field was in colour a
' desolate drab ; it was a complexion with-
' out features, as if a face, from chin to
' brow, should be only an expanse of skin.
' The sky wore, in another colour, the same
' likeness ; a white vacuity of countenance
' with the lineaments gone. So these two
' upper and nether visages confronted each
' other all day long, the white face looking
' down on the brown face, and the brown

' face looking up at the white face, without
' anything standing between them but the
' two girls crawling over the surface of the
' former like flies.'

The effects of light and flame are noted
as if he had lived for the purpose. Fires
fascinate him. The one at the Three
Tranters in 'Desperate Remedies' is excellently precise and impressive. There is the
burning of De Stancy Castle, too; and the
fire in Bathsheba's rickyard. But the bonfires on Egdon give him his best opportunity—

' Red suns and tufts of fire one by one
' began to arise, flecking the whole country
' round. They were the bonfires of other
' parishes and hamlets that were engaged in
' the same sort of commemoration. Some
' were distant, and stood in a dense atmo-
' sphere, so that bundles of pale straw-like
' beams radiated around them in the shape
' of a fan. Some were large and near, glow-
' ing scarlet red from the shade, like wounds

'in a black hide. Some were Mænades,
' with winy faces and blown hair. These
' tinctured the silent bosom of the clouds
' above them and lit up their ephemeral
' caves, which seemed henceforth to become
' scalding caldrons.' . . .

'All was unstable; quivering as leaves,
' evanescent as lightning. Shadowy eye-
' sockets, deep as those of a death's head,
' suddenly turned into pits of lustre: a lan-
' tern-jaw was cavernous, then it was shining;
' wrinkles were emphasized to ravines, or
' obliterated entirely by a changed ray.
' Nostrils were dark wells; sinews in old
' necks were gilt mouldings; things with no
' particular polish on them were glazed;
' bright objects, such as the tip of a furze-
' hook one of the men carried, were as
' glass; eyeballs glowed like little lanterns.
' Those whom Nature had depicted as
' merely quaint became grotesque, the
' grotesque became preternatural; for all
' was in extremity.'

Nature and human nature in his dramas
act and react on each other with constant
power. The mood and will of Nature now
rule the mood and fate of man, and again
Nature is defied by the spirit of man, and
conquered for the time, made to glance back
to him his own temper, smiling or gloomy.
It is interesting to divide Nature interpreters
into their two classes, those who love her and
demand no sympathy, but take her weal or
woe for theirs, so far as they can share them,
and those who claim sympathy from her,
and invent it if it be not forthcoming. Mr.
Hardy is in both classes ; still with him the
mood of Nature over the mood of man pre-
dominates.

His knowledge of the outside world is a
double one, that of a countryman and of
an artist. As to its artistic side, if the
examples have been ill chosen, readers will
find better ones in the books themselves.
His countryman's knowledge is no less certain. He has himself set down the differ-

ence between the outsiders and the intimates
of rural life in a fine passage in ' The Woodlanders '—

'The casual glimpses which the ordinary
' population bestowed upon that wondrous
' world of sap and leaves called the Hintock
' woods had been with these two, Giles and
' Marty, a clear gaze. They had been pos-
' sessed of its finer mysteries as of common-
' place knowledge; had been able to read
' its hieroglyphs as ordinary writing; to
' them the sights and sounds of night,
' winter, wind, storm, amid those dense
' boughs, which had to Grace a touch of
' the uncanny, and even of the supernatural,
' were simple occurrences whose origin, con-
' tinuance, and laws they foreknew. They
' had planted together, and together they
' had felled; together they had, with the
' run of the years, mentally collected those
' remoter signs and symbols which seen in
' few were of runic obscurity, but all together
' made an alphabet. From the light lashing

' of the twigs upon their faces when brush-
' ing through them in the dark, they could
' pronounce upon the species of the tree
' whence they stretched; from the quality
' of the wind's murmur through a bough
' they could in like manner name its sort
' afar off. They knew by a glance at a
' trunk if its heart were sound, or tainted
' with incipient decay; and by the state of
' its upper twigs the stratum that had been
' reached by its roots. The artifices of the
' seasons were seen by them from the con-
' juror's own point of view, and not from
' that of the spectator.' And to that intimacy he has himself been far admitted.

But he has something besides that is
warmer than the artist's love, tenderer than
the countryman's, a rapturous glory in the
beauty of the world as of one infinite and
magnificent certainty. He makes Tess sing
the pæan, 'O ye Sun and Moon' in a burst
of pure Pagan joy. That instinctive grateful
joy is his own throughout, though it oftener

speaks in pictures than in rhapsodies.   There
are dark chapters in Mr. Hardy's book of
the meaning of life, but the dark is not all
he knows : the beauty is just as sure.   When
Lavengro and Mr. Petulengro discourse, one
sunset, on the heath, on death, their dialogue
sums up much of the poetry and the philosophy of the Wessex novels.   Mr. Hardy's
two adverse but compatible moods might be
holding converse with each other—

' " Life is sweet, brother."

' " Do you think so ? "

' " Think so !   There's night and day,
' brother, both sweet things ; sun, moon,
' and stars, brother, all sweet things ; there is
' likewise a wind on the heath.   Life is very
' sweet, brother ; who would wish to die ? "

' " I would wish to die——"

' " . . . Wish to die, indeed !   A Romany
' Chal would wish to live for ever ! "

' " In sickness, Jasper ? "

' " There's the sun and stars, brother."

' " In blindness, Jasper ? "

' " There's the wind on the heath, brother." '

WESSEX

IX

WESSEX

IT need hardly be said that Mr. Hardy's
Wessex does not coincide with the old West
Saxon kingdom. Nor has he deliberately
chosen to call by the name any particularly
homogeneous part of the ancient division,
but rather the section covered by his own
observations. The name, in his limited
sense, was first used in *Cornhill*, in 1874,
where 'Far from the Madding Crowd' was
then running as a serial. It includes, till
now, parts of Somerset, Wiltshire, Berkshire,
Devon, and Hampshire, and the whole of
Dorset. Its area would be nearly enclosed
by a vertical line drawn from Exeter to the

Bristol Channel, thence by the coast to the mouth of the Avon and Bristol, by a line from Bristol to Reading, and another from Reading southward to the sea : the coast from Portsmouth to Exeter would be the southern boundary. These boundaries may, of course, be overstepped in future novels. The names of the counties are not used, but, instead, such divisions as South, Mid, North, Outer, Lower, and Upper Wessex. Outer Wessex has Taunton for its chief centre. Lower Wessex lies along the coast of the Bristol Channel, Upper Wessex along the south-eastern coast of Hampshire.

Love and patriotism have glorified many poorly dowered places ; but it happens that the region that had Mr. Hardy's first affections and has kept them, is one of singular variety and beauty. Its history is graven on its surface in wonderful characters. Everywhere springing up amid the new life are relics of a far back past, camps, barrows, giants' graves, stone circles, reminders of a forgotten worship, of a strenuous warfare, and of a patience and skill before which our modern conceit falls to pieces. The contrast of this long past with a present, home-like and familiar, but with no brand new crudity, counts for much in the interest of Wessex and its chronicles. Wessex life has a marvellous continuity, which may be partly accounted for by remoteness from the capital, by the agricultural and pastoral occupations, and partly by the essential character of the people. Mr. Hardy has given us the picked ones, maybe, but his is not the only evidence that they are a race of strong individuality and humour. These characteristics grafted on their ignorance, till a recent date, of the ways of the outer world, have made them a rich quarry for the student of humankind to dig in. A writer who has made close observations of peasant life in various parts of England, picks out the Dorset folks for special commendation for certain intellectual and social qualities ;

M

speaks of their wit, their ready appreciation
of irony, their 'native inbred refinement,'
their great desire for instruction, and de-
clares them to be 'neither sad nor sus-
'picious.' Barnes is more cautious in his
statements, but admits that 'if they are not
witty, they try to show themselves so'; he
has no doubt of their enjoyment of fun, and
speaks of the 'lively and sprack-witted young
'women.' A casual wanderer through the
county, with no special opportunity for
coming into intimate relations with the folk,
would at least report them to be more than
usually articulate. They are neither morose
nor abashed, and their tongues are both
ready and courteous.

Mr. Hardy uses to some extent the vocabulary, but hardly at all the dialect of the
people. Barnes in his 'Poems of Rural
Life' wrote either in the Dorsetshire speech
or in English. The novelist has his own
method of giving the spirit and preserving
the peculiarities of the speech in a way that

will be intelligible to his readers in other parts of the country. But of that I have spoken elsewhere.

With regard to the identifications of the scenes of Mr. Hardy's stories, I should say they have mostly been made by means of maps and personal recognition on the spot, and, as such, are fallible. Besides, Mr. Hardy is an artist, not a photographer: and he does not write guide-books. His accuracy in detail, where he chooses to make use of the quality, is marvellous; but every place that has served him as model or suggestion he has described by the light of imaginative insight more than of memory.

A word as to the names he uses. They, too, are of the soil. Wessex place names have been one source of his supply of family names : witness Melbury, Winterborne, Mottisfont, Venn, Chickerel, Millborne, and Troy. With regard to place-names he has followed no general rules. In ' The Trumpet Major,'

save for Overcombe, he has given the real
ones. Occasionally, as in ' The Distracted
Preacher,' he has mixed real and invented
ones. Mostly he has changed all the names,
sometimes substituting an older form as in
Shaston (Shaftesbury), Kingsbere (Bere
Regis), Wellbridge (Woolbridge), Abbot's
Cernel (Cerne Abbas), Ivell (Yeovil), St. Ald-
helm's Head (St. Alban's Head) ; sometimes
he has made a modification of the real name,
or received a suggestion from it, as in Sherton Abbas (Sherborne), Exonbury (Exeter),
Toneborough (Taunton), Emminster (Beaminster), Port Bredy (Bridport), Casterbridge
(Dorchester), Long Puddle (Piddlehentride),
Chaseborough (Cranborough), Wintoncester
(Winchester), Evershead (Evershott). Others
are outright inventions, made, of course, with
an ear for local probability.

Casterbridge is a good centre from which
to reach the scenes of many of the stories.
In one of them it is drawn with perfect art
and truth, and Mr. Hardy's own town is admirably fitted for such treatment. The

character stamped on it is not the mark of
a life that has passed into decay, but of a
sturdy present making use of and blending
with the past. The story of 'The Mayor of
Casterbridge' opens, however, with the famous
wife-selling scene at Weydon Priors—by no
means the first shady transaction that has
taken place at the old Hampshire fair of
Weyhill: Langland's 'Avaricia' tells of some
he was concerned in when 'To Wy and to
Wynchestre I went to þ faire.' Susan, the
wife, and Elizabeth-Jane, her daughter,
come back many years after, and trace
Henchard to Casterbridge. '"It is huddled
'all together; and it is shut in a by a
'square wall of trees, like a plot of gar-
'den ground by a box-edging,"' says Elizabeth-Jane, very aptly, on their approach.
Every feature, all the character, the avenues
of limes and chestnuts, the green escarp-
ments and walls, the streets, the inns,
the markets, are noted with nice precision
and perfect pictorial effect. Even to-day
this is true in spirit—'It stood, with regard

' to the wide fertile land adjoining, clean-
' cut and distinct, like a chess-board on a
' green table-cloth. The farmer's boy could
' sit under his barley-mow and pitch a stone
' into the office-window of the town-clerk;
' reapers at work among the sheaves nodded
' to acquaintances standing on the pave-
' ment-corner; the red-robed judge, when
' he condemned a sheep-stealer, pronounced
' sentence to the tune of Baa, that floated
' in at the window from the remainder of
' the flock browsing hard by.' Just outside
the town, on the Weymouth Road, is the
Ring, Maumsbury Ring, the great Roman
amphitheatre, where Henchard renewed
acquaintance with Susan. 'Melancholy,
' impressive, lonely, yet accessible from
' every part of the town, the historic circle
' was the frequent spot for appointments of
' a furtive kind,' always excepting those ' of
' happy lovers.' . . . 'Some old people said
' that at certain moments in the summer
' time, in broad daylight, persons sitting

' with a book, or dozing in the arena, had,
' on lifting their eyes, beheld the slopes
' lined with a gazing legion of Hadrian's
' soldiery as if watching the gladiatorial
' combat; and had heard the roar of their
' excited voices; that the scene would re-
' main but a moment, like a lightning flash,
' and then disappear.' The ' ancient square
' earthwork,' on which the Mayor planned
his unhappy entertainment, is Poundbury
Camp, where the annual sheep-fair is held.
The neighbourhood of Mixen Lane, the
' mildewed leaf in the sturdy and flourish-
' ing Casterbridge plant,' is recognisable
even in its happier condition of to-day, to
the east of the town, by the river, and near
the bridges. Crossing them you reach the
water-meadows and Ten Hatches, associated
with the misery of the mayor. When he
left the place at last, ' his path, like that of
' the Canadian woodsman, became part of a
' circle, of which Casterbridge formed the
' centre,' till worn out in spirit he lay down

in his old servant's hut in Egdon to die,
having ended his strange will with the command that no man should remember him.
The jail is connected with the fine story of
' The Three Strangers,' and with the terrible
scene in ' The Withered Arm.' Rhoda and
Gertrude Lodge come to their strange meeting there from the meads lower down the
river, near Stoke, in the Wareham neighbourhood. The ' ivied manor-house flanked
' by battlemented towers,' the home of the
Lady Penelope, is the old house of Wolveton, just beyond the town, on the north
side. It was into Casterbridge Union that
poor Fanny stumbled to die. But the town
has more cheerful associations. Eastward,
remoter in fact than the few miles of distance would signify, are Lewgate and Mellstock, the homes of the famous choir in
which the Dewys played their distinguished
parts. At Casterbridge statute fair, when
no man would hire him, Oak piped with
Arcadian sweetness for pence and the cheer-

ing of his heart. Into the Corn Exchange
on market-days, among the heavy yeomen,
glided fair Bathsheba, 'moved between them
' as a chaise among carts, was heard after
' them as a romance after sermons, was felt
' among them like a breeze among furnaces,'
yet intent on business, and 'holding up the
' grains in her narrow palm for inspection
' in perfect Casterbridge manner.' Her
home lay near Puddleton, the fine old house
of Waterston probably suggesting the description of the farm at Weatherbury. The
road between Weatherbury and Casterbridge
echoes with the footsteps and wheels of Mr.
Hardy's folk. Along it lies Yalbury (Yellow-
ham) Wood, scene of Dick's desperate
nutting raid, and his reconciliation with
Fancy. Some miles eastward, on the other
side of Weatherbury, looking over the little
forgotten town of Bere, is Greenhill, the
place of 'the Nijni Novgorod of Wessex,' a
waning glory now, but in its full force on
that fine September morning when Bath-

sheba's and Boldwood's flocks were driven there, and Serjeant Troy played the part of Turpin in the 'Ride to York.' It is a veritable green hill this great earthwork where the fair is held; but its name outside the novels is Woodbury. The carrier's van bearing, on that 'Saturday afternoon of blue 'and yellow autumn time,' the burden of story-telling passengers to whom we owe the 'Crusted Characters,' started from the noted bridges, and took its entertaining way to Longpuddle, which may be identified as Piddlehentride. The same highway was the scene of the 'nunny-watch,' into which his gallantry led Tony Kytes—the young man who, in return for the women's likings, 'loved 'em in shoals.' While in the neighbourhood you may trace some part of Pa'son Billy's course over Climmerston (perhaps Walterstone) Ridge to Yalbury Wood, that reckless day when Andrey and his bride, locked up in the church tower, waited in vain for parson and clerk to marry them.

One memorable feature in the neighbourhood of the town will hardly let itself be
passed by unnoticed. Merely mentioned in
' The Mayor of Casterbridge,' the great ramparts of Mai-dun, or Maiden Castle, have
hardly formed the background for any story.
Indeed, they might almost overawe a story-
teller into leaving them unused. They are the
subject of one of Mr. Hardy's finest descriptions, nevertheless, as he saw, or rather felt,
their surrounding presence one raging night
of hail and wind. In ' Earthworks at Casterbridge,' first published in an American
periodical some years ago, and reprinted in
the *English Illustrated Magazine*, December
1893, there is a little thread of grotesque story;
but in the main it is a description, needless
to say, the finest that exists, of perhaps the
most remarkable relic of past times left in
England.

The Frome Valley calls to mind not only
Tess. Lewgate and Mellstock and Stickle-
ford lie on its north side, the first two

associated with the Dewys, and all with Mop Ollamoor, 'whose fiddle would well nigh have ' drawn an ache from a gate-post.' On the road from Stinsford to Tincleton you may possibly come across them. At Anglebury, which is Wareham, at the junction of the Frome and the Puddle, Ethelberta makes her first appearance; and here her various pursuers meet, or just miss, that morning when they are severally determined to prevent her marriage with Mountclere. One of the Stoke villages not far off must mark the near neighbourhood of Lodge's dairy where Rhoda was employed, whither she returned many years after her son's tragedy in Casterbridge jail, and where 'sometimes, ' those who knew her experiences would ' stand and observe her, and wonder what ' sombre thoughts were beating inside that ' impassive, wrinkled brow, to the rhythm of ' the alternating milk-streams.'

But Rhoda's story seems more a part of Egdon Heath, near where her own hut stood,

and where Conjuror Trendle dwelt who read
her influence on Gertrude's withered arm.
The whole drama of 'The Return of the
Native' passes within a small portion of
Egdon Heath, and Egdon is the name given
to all the wild moorland between Dorchester
and Poole Harbour. It is broken now into
many parts : into Morden, and Bere, and
Wool, and Duddle, and other heaths ; but
the attempts at cultivation have met with desperate resistance, and the breaks into green
strips of cornfields slip the memory on a
back-look at that lonely land. Broader
stretches of moorland, reaching immensity,
will be found elsewhere, but the gloom,
not black, but made of a secretion of all the
rich colours of darkness, is nowhere more
intense, while the lines formed by hill and
mound and cresting barrow have, especially
in the western portion, a grandeur not
measured by height or length or any other
dimension. Its lonely face, and the face of
all heath-lands are interpreted in 'The

Return of the Native.' Mr. Hardy's sketch-map of the scene of the story, given in all save the popular editions of the book, makes clear the respective situations of Bloomsend and Alderworth, Mistover and Shadwater Weir, marks too the character of the surface, with its fringing meadows, its barrows, and sparse trees. You may look westward rather than eastward for such a tract of country, to a region where thorn-trees are a special feature of the heath; but if you fail, as is probable, to find it, it matters little, for all Egdon is haunted by the gloomy beauty of Eustacia who walks still in her prisoned discontent.

Some of the best of the stories draw us to the coast. First 'The Trumpet Major,' of course. You may look in vain now for the actual dwelling-place of the miller, and Mrs. Garland, and Anne. The old mill house at Sutton Pointz to the north-east of Weymouth—here called Weymouth, not Budmouth as in the rest of the stories—has been pulled down, and a red brick one has

recently taken its place. But the stream
is there, and the downs where the soldiers
camped, and if your imagination be worth
anything you will still see the Trumpet Major's
epaulettes and Anne's yellow gipsy hat in
the garden, and hear him speaking to her at
a discreet distance in 'deep firm accents
' across the gooseberry bushes or through the
' tall rows of flowering peas.' If you climb
the downs above the mill you may see, if
your eyes and the atmosphere permit,
what the Overcombe folks saw when they
gathered there to watch for the king :
' Weymouth and Deadman's Bay beyond,
' and Portland, lying on the sea to the left of
' these, like a great crouching animal tethered
' to the mainland. On the extreme east of
' the marine horizon, St. Alban's Head
' closed the scene, the sea to the southward
' of that point glaring like a mirror under
' the sun. Inland could be seen Badbury
' Rings [beyond Sturminster Marshall],
' where a beacon had been recently erected,
' and farther to the left Bulbarrow [over-

' looking Blackmore Vale], where another
' beacon stood. Not far from this came
' Nettlecombe Tout [to the left of Bulbar-
' row]; to the west, Dogberry Hill, and
' Black'on near to the foreground.' Black'on,
or Blackdown, is conspicuous enough now
with its tall monument to the memory of
Nelson's Hardy, to whose house at Porti-
sham Bob walked, after dodging the press-
gang, to beg from him a berth on the
Victory. North of Weymouth is little Radi-
pole, where Anne was comforted in her
grief by the king, and from whence she
departed for Overcombe with ' visions of
' Bob promoted to the rank of admiral, or
' something equally wonderful, by the king's
' special command, the chief result of the
' promotion being in her arrangement of the
' piece, that he should stay at home and go
' to sea no more.'

The same downs call up the story of ' The
Melancholy Hussar,' the sensitive Matthäus
Tina, who, love-sick for Phyllis and home-

sick for the Fatherland, planned the escape
for which he was shot as a deserter. Farther
to the east, by Lulworth Cove, Solomon
Selby, watching the ewes and the young
lambs by night, had the vision of the 'two
' men in boat cloaks, cocked hats, and
' swords,' looking at a chart of the channel
by aid of a dark lantern. One of them, with
' his bullet head, his short neck, and his
' round yaller cheeks and chin, his gloomy
' face, and his great glowing eyes,' he de-
clared to his dying day was Boney.

Admirers, and they must be many, of the
fascinating Lizzie Newberry, desiring to keep
pace with her adventures, may identify her
village of Nethermynton as Overmoyne,
on the highroad from Dorchester to Wareham. There good Mr. Stockdale, sent to
care for souls, found himself aiding and
abetting smugglers, and loving to distraction
the smuggler-in-chief, whose staggering defence was that she dissented from State as
he from Church. His on route that exciting

N

night when he pursued her unbeknown can easily be traced over the hill to Holworth, thence to the cliff above Ringworth (Ringstead) Bay. The next night when he went along with her protestingly but protectingly, their road lay over Lord's Barrow, by Chaldon Down, thence to Lullstead (Lulworth) Cove. That was the last escapade before the desperate search of the exasperated excisemen fort he ' things ' sacrilegiously stored away below Overmoyne church tower.

' Fellow Townsmen,' another coast story, has Port Bredy, which is Bridport, for its scene, ' An Imaginative Woman,' Southsea, or a seaside town in its near neighbourhood. Avice Caro's home was in Portland Isle. Knollsea, where many of the leisure moments of Ethelberta's busy scheming life were spent, is Swanage. It is the place of her hurried wedding, too, with Mountclere. From here she set out on her famous donkey-ride to the Imperial Archæological Association's meeting at Combe, otherwise Corfe Castle. On her way, standing on the Giant's

Grave, she had that magnificent view over Purbeck and the Channel, which makes one of the two or three great passages in the book. Sandbourne, the watering-place of sudden growth like the 'prophet's gourd,' ' an exotic on the borders of a prehistoric ' region where not a sod had been turned ' since the days of Cæsar,' is Bournemouth, associated with Ethelberta's and Picotee's history, but more tragically with that of Tess. Havenpool, where Joliffe gave public thanks in church for his marvellous escape, is Poole. Here his wife, after having sent him and her sons away, for her ambitious ends, waited and waited their return from the sea that never gave them up.

North from Poole you reach the picturesque old town of Warborne, Wimborne Minster, where Swithin had his schooling, a ' " place where they draw up young gam'sters' ' brains like rhubarb under a nine-penny ' pan, my lady, excusing my common way." ' The lonely tower, where he carried on his astronomical observations and Viviette's heart was captured by his beauty, might well be imaginary, but perhaps we shall not be far wrong in thinking the observatory at Horton, about five miles or so north of Wimborne, gave the first suggestion of it. Chene Manor, from which Barbara, of the House of Grebe, escaped to join young Willowes, stood where now stands Canford Magna, rather more than a mile to the south of Wimborne. Ten miles north, on the same road, was and is Lord Uplandtowers' place of St. Giles. Shottsford Forum, the home of Willowes, the glass-painter's son, is Blandford, ' where the art lingered on when it had died ' out in every other part of England.' Lornton Inn, where Willowes met Barbara on the night of the elopement, and where Lord Uplandtowers found her waiting vainly for her husband the day he was to have come home from his travels a cultivated gentleman, is Horton Inn, ' between the Forest and the Chase.' Continuing on the same road and crossing into the next county you

reach Melchester, easily recognisable as
Salisbury, which has a part in many of the
stories. There Fancy made the mistake
between All Saints and All Souls that cost
her her marriage with Troy. Viviette
married its bishop, though her heart was
with Swithin. Raye had his strange meeting
there with Edith Harnham, when he was 'on
' the Western Circuit '; and there Mountclere
tested Ethelberta's feelings for Julian, organist
in the Cathedral, so roughly as to nearly lose
her. Angel and Tess passed through it on
their way to Stonehenge.

The Hintocks, Great and Little, of 'The
' Woodlanders,' may be looked for in the
neighbourhood of the Minternes, on the
road from the county town to Sherborne.
Here, among the trees that made a friendly
home to Giles and Marty, Felice, down in
the deep shrouded glen, fretted her life out,
and for very loneliness stole the heart of
Grace's husband. Buckland Fitzpiers, perhaps Okeford St. Pain, the home of the

aristocratic ancestors of Grace's husband,
lies across Blackmore Vale, and to the south-
west of it is Middleton Abbey (Milton
Abbas), whither Felice drew the infatuated
surgeon, his wife watching him ride off into
the vale and over the high plateau, its
southern boundary, visible afar on his white
horse; while moving up the valley to her
came the loyal Giles from his cider-making,
looking and smelling like 'autumn's very
' brother.' The Woodlanders' market-town
is not Casterbridge, but Sherton, six miles
off. Here Marty sells her beautiful hair;
Giles meets his old love, returned a fine lady
from school. From the height of the windows of the Earl of Wessex and her honeymoon dignity, she looks down on him with
his cider-press and specimen apple-tree; and in
the Abbey aisles near by they walk together,
when through sorrow she has found out all
she has lost by her worldly marriage. As
has been noted in another chapter, Sherborne is also the scene of the Lady Baxby
story in the ' Noble Dames.'

To the Hintock villages, by Long Ash Lane
—part of the north road from Casterbridge,
'once a highway to Queen Elizabeth's court,'
yet so narrow that 'the brambles of the
'hedge, which hung forward like anglers'
'rods over a stream, scratched their hats
'and curry-combed their whiskers, as they
'passed,' Darton and Japheth Johns
journeyed on the unfortunate courting ex-
pedition to the Knap. King's Hintock Court,
'one of the most imposing of the mansions
'that overlook our beautiful Blackmoor or
'Blakemore Vale,' is Melbury House. Here
Betty Dornell lived with her mother, the
heiress of the Strangways, with her father
too, save when he quarrelled with his
ambitious wife and rode off to his own place
of Falls, twenty miles away on the other side
of Ivell (Yeovil). Falls is Mells Park, in
Somerset. Between the two houses plays
the story, save for the visit to London
where the child-marriage took place, and
for the journey to Bristol, where the puff-

ing angry squire met his courtly son-in-law.

In following the fortunes of Tess, you pass over a good part of the county. Marlott, her early home, lies in Blackmore Vale, 'where the fields are never brown and the ' springs never dry,' between Stourminster and Shaftesbury. Her search for fortune at the bidding of her family, led her to Trantridge, near Chaseborough, the home of the sham D'Urbervilles, possibly Pentridge, near Cranbourne, a place identified too, with the interesting 'incident in the life of Mr. George ' Crookhill.' After her sad home-coming, when the forces of her nature revived again, she set off once more 'on a thyme-scented, ' bird-hatching morning in May,' south this time, by Stourminster, Weatherbury (Puddletown), over part of Egdon, to the valley of the Great Dairies. Sorrow has its home there as elsewhere, but there is something fitting in making the sparkling Frome Valley, with its flocks of browsing kine, its pure streams, its wealth of flowers, the scene of the renewal of Tess's hopefulness. On the eventful ride with the milk-pails to Wellbridge (Wool), Angel and Tess passed the 'fragment of the old manor house of Caroline ' date,' that was to have such an effect on her fortunes. Here she came as a bride to this home of her ancestors, Old Woolbridge House, spoken of elsewhere. Out of the green meadows and shining waters rises gray and hoary. Its crumbling decay gave the atmosphere that heightened Angel's melancholy, and the wicked pictures inside, with their suggestions of a bad inheritance in Tess, made much of whatever case he had. The mill, where he was a temporary pupil, lies along the stream eastward, by Bindon Abbey, amid the ruins of which is the graveyard with the abbot's tomb, in which he laid her in the sleep-walking scene. Her way home after their separation lay by Weatherbury (Puddletown), Nuzzlebury (Haselbury Bryan), and thence into the Vale.

Her wanderings then began anew, first to Port Bredy (Bridport), afterwards to the upland farm at Flintcomb Ash, in the centre of the county. The bare, unkindly place, where the maturer Tess felt, not for the first time, the sorrow, but all the hardness of life, is in the neighbourhood of Plush. No wonder Marion and she would look south-eastward to the Var valley, where they had known kindlier days. When she was sent off with the blessings and the proud touches of Marion and Izz, on the visit to Angel's home, her road lay first northward to the boundary ridge of the Vale, then westward above the Minternes (I give the probable translations of the names where necessary, for all are not disguised), skirting High Stoy, to Cross in Hand, near the boundary of Sydling and Batcombe parishes, where the stone pillar with the hand carved on it 'stands desolate and silent, to mark the site ' of a miracle or murder, or both.' Farther on she crossed Long Ash Lane, and dipped down to Evershott, then westward through a gentler country by Benville Lane to Beaminster, where Parson Clare ministered. Frightened by the overheard words of Mercy Chant and the brothers Clare, she took the fifteen mile road back again, without fulfilling her errand. It was at Evershott she recognised Alec D'Urberville in the ranting preacher, and at the old pagan monument of Cross in Hand, he made her swear, with a strange irony, never to tempt him from his mission by her charms. Family troubles brought her to Marlott again, and turned the Durbeyfields adrift on the world. They sought a new home at Kingsbere (Bere Regis), an earlier possession of their ancestors than Woolbridge. It was on Old Lady Day they made the move, meeting 'many other ' waggons with families on the summit of ' the load, which was built on a well-nigh ' unvarying principle, as peculiar, probably, ' to the rural labourer, as the hexagon to the ' bee. The ground-work of the arrangement

' was the family dresser, which, with its
' shining handles, and finger marks, and
' domestic evidences thick upon it, stood
' importantly in front, over the tails of the
' shaft-horses, in its erect and natural position,
' like some Ark of the Covenant that they
' were bound to carry reverently.' Mr. Hardy
has described the same scene elsewhere,
in his article on 'The Dorset Labourer';
and the sight is indeed a striking one,
strangely compounded of melancholy and
hope. Under the churchyard wall of 'the
' half-dead townlet' of Bere, the waggon was
unloaded, since D'Urberville, to gain his
private ends, had frustrated their plan of
taking lodgings. By the south wall of the
fine old church, the family tester was set up,
under the traceried window of many lights,
blazoned with the names and arms of the
Turbervilles. The ubiquitous villain turned
up ; the family were saved from penury, and
Tess's tragedy moved fast. She passed then
to Sandbourne, that is, Bournemouth. Her

escape with Angel lay north through the New Forest to Salisbury and Stonehenge. The last scene of all was at Winchester, out of which Angel and Liza-Lu walked hand-in-hand.

Winchester plays a part in a minor drama. In the most convenient of towns 'for medi- 'tative people to live in; since there you 'have a Cathedral with a nave so long that 'it affords space in which to walk and summon 'your remoter moods without continually 'turning on your heel, or seeming to do more 'than take an afternoon stroll under cover 'from the rain and the sun,' there, in the Cathedral itself, did Sir Ashley Mottisfont ask in marriage Philippa, 'the gentle daughter 'of plain Squire Okehall'; and thus made a home, for the time, for the poor shuttle-cocked Dorothy.

Near Aldbrickham (Reading) lies the village whence Sophy was taken out of her sphere to which she would fain have returned, had not her rigid son put his veto on her marriage with the honest greengrocer. To other outlying parts, Toneborough and Exonbury (Taunton and Exeter), Mr. Millborne returned to expiate his youthful wrong-doing, an expiation which had consequences of a kind to shake the foundations of any ordinary conscience. The Lady Icenway hailed from this side too, from 'one o' the greenest bit ' of woodlands between Bristol and the city ' of Exonbury,' and the Honourable Laura's adventures took place on the wild north coast of Lower Wessex.

Thus, through the Wessex novels we trudge many roads, and through varied landscapes. And if the mere identification of localities be but of minor interest, in the course of it there is abundant illustration of the part that scene and landscape play in Mr. Hardy's dramas, a part of much consequence to the characters, and often hardly subordinate to them.

POINT OF VIEW

X

POINT OF VIEW

It is an unsatisfactory kind of homage to attempt to construct a complex system of thought from a novelist's pictures of life. He can retort on your blunders by saying he only holds up a mirror and catches reflections. But, at least, the mind and the eye and the angle of vision concern the reflections. And Mr. Hardy has a special point of view, by which I do not mean a theory of art, but a theory of life at least consistent enough to give an interest to his work apart from its artistic value. To treat the Wessex novels merely as scenic and dramatic representations is to ignore one of their vital characteristics. This point of view is not

o

completely expounded. It is a matter of temperament perhaps as much as of opinion ; but it asserts itself with a pervasive force from which no reader can escape.

To call him pessimist is short and easy; only it hides half the truth. He is so, of course, but with a difference. Yet in insisting on the difference one cannot slur over the pessimism ; he is particularly emphatic about it himself. From his survey of the world he has concluded that life is gay only so long as its conditions are unknown, that real happiness is incompatible with fearless thought and the knowledge that science has made common property of the shortcomings of natural laws, which cripple human powers, and the defects of which no human devotion can remedy. It is noticeable that to almost all his tragic characters he has given the power and habit of thinking. There are darker views of the present compatible with a different conclusion, if the ills of life are held to be not the necessary symptoms of faulty laws of nature, but of a rotten social system, curable by time and revolution and the inculcation of a keener sense of moral responsibility. Mr. Hardy would probably use 'alleviation' instead of 'cure,' though his pessimism has never taken away his belief in the usefulness of human struggle. You will find many utterances scattered up and down his writings sympathetic with the reforming spirit; and 'Tess' is, of course, a defiant challenge to the world to revise a cruel social code—a defiance which despair alone could not emit.

Never did a novelist feel less compelled to invent happy endings. He would say he invents no endings, but gives the natural ones, according to his experience of life. Clym's life is wrecked by an unselfish and inevitable devotion to what was alien to him; Troy has the love of women, not John, or Giles; Gabriel only comes to his own after the zest of life has departed from him and Bathsheba; the Mayor dies alone in poverty after efforts that Farfrae would never need to make ; Marty is left with a grave to keep ; the repentance of Millborne brings his ruin ; Tess, born for sheltered domesticity, dies a felon's death.   Examples come thickly on the memory.   Mr. Hardy's emphatic lack of cheerful complacency in his final view of life has effectually barred his way to a very wide popularity—

> *haec ratio plerumque videtur tristior esse quibus non est tractata, retroque volgus abhorret ab hac.*

The sum of his reflections, and the conclusion to be drawn from his examples, are not gay.   But they are not dispiriting, and never brought on a coward mood.   The only really dispiriting thing in the world is cynicism, and though satire and bitter irony are frequent with Mr. Hardy, of cynicism he utters not a word.   The tragic, his deepest note, is furthest of all from the cynical, for it recognises in the fragile, battered thing called life the stirrings and impulses of greatness.   Life

is not little, nor cheap, nor easily found out.
And its path is lined with interest. Since it
has to be walked, why shut your eyes to the
excellent entertainment by the way? The
permutations and combinations of human
motive and instinct and conduct are infinite. Its problems and dramas are innumerable; your simplest neighbour has an
ocean of the unexpected in him, and provides continual comedy. If the novelist has
any clear moral duty to perform, it is to show
that life is strong enough in interest to make
it worth while living. This Mr. Hardy has
done abundantly. And not only has he
shown it as full of interest, but also of
beauty. The road to dusty death is warmed
by the sun; the sap rises in the wayside trees
every year; the spring wind on the down,
the fresh life in the grass, are, while experience of them lasts, just as real as sorrow, and
it would be the foolishest asceticism that
would shut the doors of the heart on them.
There is another reality, too, the need in a

vexing world of sympathy; and thus all
reasons for cynicism are taken away.   Mr.
Hardy has faced the sadness of life, and
spoken it.   We may wish he had felt less
cause to express it so frequently.   He cannot
offer, as does his countryman Barnes, the
consolation in the dream of 'a year that 's
' winterless, where glassy waters never vroze.'
But, even for those who accept his conclusions as truth, by urging and proving the
interest and beauty of the world he has taken
the worst part of the curse away.

And his pessimism does not mean a placid
acceptance of the ills of life.   The patience,
or it may be, the low vitality, that marks
some sad-voiced exponents of the view, is
not his.   You never feel enervated as after
a course of Russian fiction.   He is often in
revolt: otherwise he would be no tragedian.
Perhaps placidity and indifference would be
more logical in the looker-on at so imperfect
a world; but men of vigour are not made
that way.   Human nature and Nature's laws

are so little in accord that the complete sub-
jection of the heart and tongue of man is
impossible except from sheer fatigue. He
will not mock at the creatures who sin and
suffer in consequence of decrees misunder-
stood or contradictory. In his revolt and in
his resignation he cries to whatever powers
may be,

'For all the sin wherewith the Face of Man
  Is blackened—Man's forgiveness give—and take ! '

Save where men continue to thwart and
narrow the remaining chances of life, he takes
side with humanity against the Olympians.

Mr. Hardy is not a moralist. But inferentially he inculcates some things that are
of importance to morality, and nearly all of
these, when applied, are weapons hurled at
the conventions. The hatefulness of cant
everywhere, but especially in morals, where
no rule-of-thumb is of service, but heart and
mind must continually be exercised ; the
cowardice of mere propriety, and all obedi-
ence to something learnt in other circum-

stances instead of something felt in these ;
the cruelty of class prejudice, he has abundantly satirised.   And, on this moral side,
it is of particular interest to note in a novelist
whose frequent theme is the caprice, the
weakness, the wandering nature of humankind, his unshaken faith in the power that
the ideal has over human hearts, over the
elect, who will always be few, but who will not
fail, from one generation to another.   He is
never sceptical about the power of spiritual
reward, seeming to regard the 'absolute
' gratuitousness' of any ideal act, like Mr.
Millborne's reparation, in ' For Conscience
' Sake,' ' as being a special inducement to per-
' form it.'   Indeed there is a rare mixture of
hope and belief in Mr. Hardy's dark views.
His humanism is not merely an intellectual
or dramatic interest in the doings and motives
of men ; with it are mingled trust and sympathy.   Man's nature is, as he says, in what
reads like a fine version of Pascal, ' neither
' ghastly, hateful, nor ugly ; neither common-

' place, unmeaning, nor tame, but . . . slighted
' and enduring ; and withal singularly colossal
' and mysterious.' The troubles of men he
will not always treat as sordid maladies, but
as honourable scars, ' *misères de grand sei-*
' *gneur.*' He has laughed at human nature,
but he has never belittled it.

So much for the temper underlying his
more serious work. But in the material
which he uses to show the tragedy and the
comedy of life his point of view is just as
much involved. Mr. Hardy recognises, without apology, the passion in human nature in
a franker way than any of the other greater
English novelists save the two elder Brontës.
Till recently, English fiction was singularly
lacking in its delineation, or in the presentment of the moral questions of which it is
the source. Where strong passions form the
motives of stories in the great period, as they
do, scenically, in Scott, and with more personal intensity in Thackeray, they are mostly
imagined on conventional lines, and as paying

due deference to social laws. This is perhaps
the normal condition of things. Very likely
we shall come back to it when the old order
is reaccepted, or a new one established.
But the fiction of a day when every law is
weighed in the balance, and many are found
wanting, is bound to be morally experi-
mental and turbulent. Scott and Thackeray
lived in stirring enough times, but the fer-
ments then were political rather than moral.
The forces of the Revolution first touched,
for a few, poetry, for the many, politics.
Only a small number of peculiarly impres-
sionable souls, like Shelley, were stirred to
investigate and question the adequacy of the
accepted moral code. Practical England had
settled that long ago in a way no scatter-
brained poet could disturb. The wave of
change swept into the political world, swamp-
ing, disintegrating, with a long, steady force,
and then into the religious one no less
strongly. It has reached the world of morals
at last.

The recognition of the right, or, at least, of the might, of passion, and of the importance of sexual questions in modern English novels, are two parallel but widely different facts. Unhappily, only the latter is real to any very great extent. The problems of the sexes are of keen present interest, affecting as they do everybody to some extent. The solutions attempted, and the examples presented, are often false and frivolous, but the interest they represent is real enough, a fatiguing reality, perhaps, but one that has to be faced till the intelligent acceptance of some code, old or new, be a general fact. Stories of great passions are common, too, as blackberries, but it is not only their presentment that is artificial. They are mostly hollow altogether. For passion, the genius of the human heart, is by no means a common thing. Perhaps not only in appearance, but in fact, is the English race passionless, with capacities for breeding great exceptions. Even in our earlier fiction, which was assuredly far from reticent, it is by no means a conspicuous note. The dramatists chose their examples mostly from warmer skies, and it was only rare natures they endowed with the capacity, not the average men and women born in the brain of average novelists. It exists, nevertheless, among a cold and a practical people, and though the taboo has not been taken off its expression, it is recognised, with feverish feebleness, by many, and with the direct force that belongs to it by a few. In the social ferment it has been rediscovered as a tremendous human power existing in life, rarely but very really, outside poetry, this very day as well as in the early world, material for fiction as well as for opera.

In considering France, the other principal fiction-producing country, it would be absurd to name the social ferment as bringing passion, with the moral questions involved, into prominence. It has never sought justification there. And the second influence on our freer-spoken novel of to-day is, of course, a French one. This is not the place to acknowledge our literary debt to France. It is enough to say that French novelists emphasised the fact that English ones were missing great human chances by keeping whole chapters of the book of life unwritten —chapters just as moral or non-moral as the others already disclosed. The gratitude of English readers for the greater frankness and wider compass of French fiction has too often ended in indiscriminating admiration. A native manufacture of the thing has been set up from an English translation of the French receipt. The supply is hardly a matter for congratulation. For the passion and the revolt from conventional morals in modern French literature are not mere frank recognitions of a reality. The thing is absurdly overdone. It has swamped the rest of life's interests. It has become partly a trick and partly a mania, and it ends by boring us inextinguishably till we are ready to put up equal claims for any of the other human activities as material for the novelist, for money-getting, tiger-hunting, gold-digging, prize-fighting, or horse-racing. Needless to say, the great writers of fiction have hardly ever left us in this mood, for they have that essential sincerity which in an artistic sense is the concomitant of supreme talent. But the detestablest thing on earth is simulated passion; the most unwholesome, the stupidest, its manufacture for trade purposes. And one of the chief inconveniences of this cheap erotic fiction, and of the handling of delicate moral problems by bunglers, is that for a time, long enough to cause annoyance, the false is confused with the real and brings on it reproach. For the weak dabblers in this dangerous research the real students, with their fingers on human hearts and pulses, are made responsible. Mr. Hardy has suffered in this way.

From the beginning he sounded the note of human passion. The persons in the fore-

ground of his dramas are chosen from beyond the commonplace, and they mostly play
their parts in ' those sequestered spots out-
' side the gates of the world, where may
' usually be found more meditation than
' action, and more listlessness than medita-
' tion ; where reasoning proceeds on narrow
' premises, and results in inferences wildly
' imaginative ; yet where, from time to time,
' dramas of a grandeur and unity truly Sopho-
' clean, are enacted in the real, by virtue of
' the concentrated passions and closely-knit
' interdependence of the lives therein.' In
' Tess,' it takes a more prominent place
only because there it is argued about. Probably Mr. Hardy's point of view has altered
little. That his passions are realities has
never been challenged, and it has never been
stated in so many words that he should not
deal with love at white heat, only that he
might slur or veil its expression a little more.
It is an old contest, which it is best to leave
as a choice or a question. Mr. Hardy pre-

fers frankness. But good taste is compatible
with a large degree of frankness, and considering his unconventional views, and the
boldness of his ventures, his reticence is
much more remarkable than his freedom.
And his claim, implied and expressed, for
liberty of speech he has not abused. The
chronicling of sordid detail, the childish
pride in being audacious and outrageous,
are not temptations for him. Perhaps there
is no novelist with whom a love of beauty
has been a more persistent force : it has
kept him in wholesome ways. Acciden-
tal horrors and uglinesses have hardly any
place in his work at all. Only, where a thing
touches human life closely enough to make
it worth representation in a story, it has been
thought worthy of truthful expression. If it
be a warm thing, a warm word is used, and
he is not much concerned whether it be in
drawing-room vocabularies or not. In the
criticisms of Mr. Hardy's work the word
' coarse ' occurs from time to time applied

o his language. The instances are not many
vhere one could identify the words com-
)lained of unless by assuming a rigidly con-
'entional mood. The main point is that, if
dentified, they are found not to be used idly.
I'hey are finger-posts to a reality which
)therwise the timid reader would slur, and
or slurring or shrinking this novelist very
nuch in earnest has no desire. Mr. Hardy
1as never skulked.

The second request made of story-writers
vho deal in the inconvenient thing called
)assion, is that they should show up its in-
:onvenience, and indeed give it adequate
)unishment. Now, although Mr. Hardy
vould not often be in a mood to oblige this
cind of critic, he is bound to be in agreement
vith him here. For passion is so unsatisfied
ind eternally tragic a thing, hurting itself
igainst circumstances too narrow to contain
t, thrust back and foiled continually, that
)ain is its twin-brother, even though it burst
nto no wild deed calling for the exercise of

the law. The immortals have arranged all
that. In some modern English novels held
to be particularly elevating, the hero or
heroine after giving way to the inundations
of passion reappears when the wave has
passed, never a penny the better or worse or
different. Such ignorance of the ravages as
of the exaltation of passion is an immorality
of which Mr. Hardy is quite incapable. It
is no plaything with him. Boldwood, Tess,
Clym, Eustacia, and its other victims, pay
the full penalty always, because human laws
demand it, and he cannot save them. But
he has great pity for those for whom the
world has little mercy.

The justification or glorification of passion
is, however, not the most serious criticism
that has been brought against him. He is
charged with a preference for such subjects
as stimulate the senses. This is worth while
bringing to proof, and one looks over the
novels to see what character to give over to
the severities of the censor, and what situa-

ions one would like to reconstruct on a more
noral basis. Surely Miss Aldclyffe, poor
storm-tossed soul, may be left in peace. Lord
Mountclere is a disagreeable old gentleman
of a conventional type, but his path was not
in easy one after he married Ethelberta. De
Stancy is certainly unwholesome. One is
nclined to make him the scapegoat, place
he highly respectable book in which he
igures on the Index, and enjoy this outrage
on the proprieties of Paula and Somerset.
Viviette is not healthy in soul : in that her
innatural circumstances have their natural
consequence. The Noble Dames are of a
lay of freer manners than ours, but their
reedoms are scrupulously translated into
vords that will offend as little as possible the
straiter morals of the present. Charles Raye
of 'On the Western Circuit,' stands out
eadier than most for absolute condemnation;
out he is expressly treated as no hero : only
i little pity is shown him in the strange situa-
ion into which, by an unforeseen path, his

fault has led him. Alec D'Urberville, the type of sensuality in its most undiluted form, is surely an awful warning ; and is poor Tess, because her heart was surcharged with a good thing, and her person had attractions which, being of moment in her history, are chronicled, to be held accurst ? She can suggest evil thoughts only to the vile. Yet, to be candid, in the search for instances to support the criticism, one must own to finding a good deal that is, at least, morbid.

Mr. Hardy is certainly not coerced by the influences of his time, but certain features of it he reflects ; the psychology of love is a study of the day, and the neurotic and the abnormal have inevitable attractions for the student of the workings of the human mind. From this scientific interest spring 'Squire Petrick's Lady,' 'On the Western Circuit,' and 'An Imaginative Woman.' The only way to escape from the influence is to write of wild adventure, to use love superficially as a mere starting-point or goal, of no real interest in the actual running of the romance. Excellent things are these tales of adventure, but not what he was called to write. And the head and front of his offending is that, more from his hatred of the commonplace than his preference for the morbid, he has put some of his men and women in strange situations, where wholesome thoughts could hardly grow, and that, when the animal nature or superficial attractions, apart from the heart and brain, have been the motive power, he has said so. He has dissected mental maladies without bungling; he has not exaggerated them, though they are a more frequent theme in his later books. The only real immorality possible in art is untruth. Mr. Hardy out of unhealthy soil makes strange growths proceed. To lack of restraint and sin he may not always give the pedagogic punishment the moralist might dictate, but they have their inevitable and adequate consequence. Social law may be held in contempt, but it is never ignored.

Against this morbidity must be placed at least two-thirds of his work, all his utterance of the laughter of life, of the beauty of the face of the outer world, and his delicate portrayal of that other human nature whose emotions live in an atmosphere of cool, transparent purity, untempted from within, simple, patient and staunch. Dick Dewy, Gabriel, Giles, Marty, Elizabeth-Jane, are as real as Troy and Eustacia, and as characteristic of the mind of their maker. Only, he refuses to condemn passion, or even to apologise for it; indeed, justifies it, or any other strong impulse of nature till it be proved by reason, not convention, cruel and antisocial in its indulgence. There are uses for every natural force, and though asceticism and Puritanism, and every repressing creed and code have borne flowers fair and fine, that does not alter the fact that nature will be corrupted rather more than less by starvation and an underground life.

This claim for greater freedom to man's

nature does not, as has been seen, accom
pany a very light-hearted view of things. His
occasional grim earnestness, his intellectual
cast of mind, his brooding thoughtfulness,
his austerity, make all the more remarkable
his clear perception of the comedy in life.
His tolerance, indeed his enjoyment, of
caprice and vanity and all the feather-headed
human moods and ways, if only they be
young and graceful, may seem difficult to fit
in with his theory of the world. But in
truth they are the woof-threads of a sane
and liveable philosophy.

The observations on men and things
scattered in reflections about his novels, or
translated into characters and incidents, are
not of the kind best learnt in social assem-
blies. The shrewdness of the man of the
world is very little evident. He has scanned
human features as well as hearts with keenest
gaze, and his intercourse with men seems
never to have been languid. But his best
thought reflects a mind that has lived its

intensest life apart. He is independent and profound rather than brilliant. It is just this aloofness, revealing itself in wisdom and in beauty that have had leisure and quiet to grow in, that has given coherence and con sistency to his novels, and made it worth while trying to examine his point of view at all.

Not that he has posed as philosopher, or even as poet. Indeed, it is hardly fitting to force him into either part, and thus take leave of him. Story-teller, picture-maker, humourist, it is entertainment he offers us. Only, the stories he has heard, and imagined, and told us, have interpreted life to him, and he lets us overhear the commentary sometimes. And behind his vivid representations of the human comedy is visible something greater : a poetic intention which his art has abundantly fulfilled.

www.ingramcontent.com/pod-product-compliance
Lightning Source LLC
Chambersburg PA
CBHW020109030726
47498CB00006B/2027